Books by L.

Tales from The Edge

Reaching the Edge
Living on the Edge
Dancing on the Edge
A Double-Edged Sword
Rough Around the Edges
Scorched Edges

Investigating Love

Rasputin's Kiss
Evil's Embrace
Tarot's Touch

The Wyverns

Mantrap
Deathtrap
Rattrap

Warlocks

Elemental Love

Sexy Snax

Black Dog

What's His Passion?

Testing Lysander
What's His Passion?

Picturing Lysander

Anthologies

Hard Riders
Racing Hearts
His Rules

Single Titles

The Portrait
Mountain Rescue
Stroke Rate
Chemical Bonds
Tagging Mackenzie

Rasputin's Kiss

ISBN # 978-1-78651-918-4

©Copyright L.M. Somerton 2016

Cover Art by Posh Gosh ©Copyright 2016

Interior text design by Claire Siemaszkiewicz

Pride Publishing

Published in 2016 by Pride Publishing, Newland House, The Point, Weaver Road, Lincoln, LN6 3QN, United Kingdom.

Printed in Great Britain by Clays Ltd, St Ives plc
1

Investigating Love

RASPUTIN'S KISS

L.M. SOMERTON

Dedication

To all my readers who have been with me since the
beginning of this adventure.

Chapter One

Inspector Alex Courtney paced back and forth across the silent incident room like a caged tiger with an attitude problem. He didn't lose his temper often, but he was getting dangerously close to a firework display to rival New Year over the Sydney Harbour Bridge. He raked his fingers through hair that already stuck up wildly then loosened his tie, which threatened to strangle him. He muttered and cursed under his breath before he spoke out loud, "Nothing! We've got nothing! That's four murders in the last six months — this psycho's fucking playing with us and he's winning the damn game." Alex stared blindly at the large pin board that took up almost the entire length of one wall.

Four young faces gazed accusingly back at him. Four young men who had been ripped from their lives, slaughtered and dumped like garbage. Alex knew them all inside out, their faults and qualities, their ruined hopes and dreams, the desperation and grief of their families and friends. So much energy and potential removed from the world. Every death cut him to the core.

He slammed his fist against the wall in frustration then spun around to witness several of his team, who were collectively attempting to be inconspicuous, wincing in sympathy with his abused hand. Chips of plaster and flecks of dust rained onto the floor. Self-inflicted pain diffused his rage and, much more quickly than it had built, all the tension dissipated from Alex's lean six feet, three inch frame. He ground the heels of his hands into his eye sockets, attempting to rub away some of the exhaustion that came from weeks of marathon working hours and little sleep. He knew the action would do nothing to soften the deep black circles that sat beneath his eyes. It was getting so that he was afraid to look in his bathroom mirror in the mornings, his reflection was that scary.

He surveyed his team, all looking just as tired and haggard as he was. "Okay. I have an idea that I want to run by you, but it'll sit better on full stomachs. Give me ten minutes to do a run to the canteen. Someone put the kettle on, because you're going to need strong coffee too." Alex used the short walk to and from the staff canteen to play the idea he'd been working on over and over his mind, testing options and possibilities. It was a bit radical, but that was what the case needed — something that pushed the boundaries of the investigation.

Having made a decision about what he was going to do next, Alex felt more relaxed than he had in an age.

He was a little anxious about how the team would react to his plan but when it came down to it, he was in charge and they would have to go along with it whether they liked it or not. Still, he would much rather have their whole-hearted support. He knew they were as frustrated as he was about the lack of a break in the case, so maybe his idea wouldn't be shot down in flames. He returned to the incident room with a determined set to his shoulders. Steaming mugs of strong coffee had already been handed out and Alex distributed the bacon sandwiches that he had liberated from the canteen. Okay, so it was a bribe. Advanced payment to offset the grief he knew he was about to get. At least they'd be laughing at him with satisfied stomachs.

Alex ignored the suspicious glances that flashed between his team members like some kind of semaphore.

"What's up now then, boss? Don't tell me... We've got some fucking journalist ride-along?" That had come from his veteran sergeant, Higgs.

"Nah. That can't be it, Sarge. That's not worth bacon butties. It must be something much worse." Detective Pete

Harris looked thoughtful. "The Chief Inspector is up the duff and the boss is responsible." That got a few snorts of laughter in response.

"The Chief may come across as holier than thou, Pete, but even she couldn't manage the Immaculate Conception," Alex retorted from his perch on the edge of a desk. He let the banter continue for a minute or two then broke in, "Can it, you lot. Even if I were inclined to switch teams, which I'm not, Chief Inspector Mary Sissons would hardly be my first port of call. She's old enough to be my fucking mother!"

His team dissolved into guffaws of laughter and Alex smiled. "It saddens me deeply that I can't do something nice for you without aspersions of guilt being cast on my character. I'm deeply hurt."

The sergeant slurped his coffee. "The last time you bought us breakfast, guv, you told us the overtime budget had been cut. You can't blame us for being suspicious. Besides, we're detectives. We're supposed to read between the lines of every situation and you did say you had a plan."

Alex gave a wry smile. "Well, that is true. However, this morning has absolutely nothing to do with overtime, I promise. I've been doing some thinking..."

That brought another chorus of groans and sarcastic comments.

Alex rolled his eyes. "Yes, it does occasionally happen. Even to senior officers. Anyway, I've decided to take a new tack with this investigation. We are going to try something different. We need bait." He paused to let that sink in.

"What do you mean by bait, exactly?" Phil Cole, the youngest member of his team other than Alex himself fanned his face anxiously then loosened his tie and undid the button at his collar.

"Don't worry, Phil, your arse is safe. You're too old and nowhere near pretty enough for our resident psychopath." Cole looked relieved rather than insulted and chewed on his sandwich. "So if not me, then who?"

Alex steeled himself. "I never thought I'd hear myself

saying this to you lot"—he cast an eye over the four men that made up his team—"but I want you to find me a boyfriend."

It was a great indication of the respect that Alex had earned from his team that the laughter that followed was not too hysterical. There was some choking and a couple of creative swear words, but other than that his colleagues were remarkably controlled.

"I know you're laughing with me, not at me, but if you've got that initial reaction out of your systems, perhaps you could tell me what you think. Am I way off the mark with this?"

The room got quiet for a while as they thought about the idea.

"Okay, boss. Exactly what, or who, are we looking for?" It was grizzled Sergeant Higgs that spoke up first. He had thirty years on the job and was never fazed by anything.

"It's not going to be easy." Alex gestured at the incident board. "He's got to tempt our killer so that means young—under twenty-five—or he has to look that way. At least six feet tall, dark-haired and good-looking. That's the profile."

"And gay?" Higgs asked.

"Not necessarily, Sarge, but if he isn't he'll need to be a bloody good actor. Oh, and he has to be in the force, no civilians. This is going to be risky."

"Christ, guv, you're not asking for much!"

Alex had already tried to think of a likely candidate but hadn't managed to come up with anyone. The local force did not recruit potential policemen because of their looks. He was hoping someone else on the team might get inspired.

There was silence as they all racked their brains for suitable candidates.

"What about P.C. Arnold?"

"He's only five feet six—what would you do? Put him on stilts?"

"Freddie Muir? He's in the right age group."

"He's about as good-looking as your dog."

"What the hell counts as good-looking? I only ogle girls!"

"Who's that new bloke in traffic? Sid something or other?"

"He couldn't look under twenty-five even if he had a facelift."

Then Sergeant Higgs muttered under his breath, "He might do. I don't know why I didn't think of him sooner." He drummed his fingers on the edge of the table and looked very pleased with himself. "Yes, definitely."

Alex rolled his eyes and gave an exaggerated sigh. "Higgs, are you going to tell the rest of us, or keep this mystery man a secret?"

Higgs grinned. "Best I just show you, boss." He got to his feet and headed for the door.

"What? Are you telling me he's in the building? Why the hell haven't I come across him then?" Alex thought he knew most of the people that worked at the station and surely he would have given a second look to someone young and handsome. He was professional but he wasn't dead and that meant he wasn't immune to a pretty face.

"From what I understand, he transferred here fairly recently and I don't think his boss lets him out much," Sarge commented. "You'll understand in a bit. Come on."

"What about us, Sarge? I think we should all get a look, don't you?"

"You're not scoring a fucking beauty pageant! Break's over. If he's any good, you'll see him soon enough." Grumbling, the rest of the team returned to their desks and Alex followed Higgs as he led him to the stairwell.

They headed downwards, but when they got to the lower ground floor Higgs kept going. Alex knew there were at least two levels underneath the building, something that was quite normal for a police station, but he had never been down any farther than the basement where the evidence room was situated. The sub-basement below that housed storage areas for archives, ammunition, confiscated drugs and other contraband — anything that needed to be kept secure. It was dark, unheated and ruled over by a sergeant the men less than fondly referred to as the devil incarnate. A shift in 'the dungeon' was often threatened as punishment for late paperwork or other misdemeanors and it was telling that the station had the best administrative record in the division.

Alex shivered as they walked along a grim, gray corridor. "Higgs, I appreciate the thought, but Sergeant 'Satan' Smith is middle-aged, balding and homophobic. He hates my guts. I don't think he'd agree to play my boyfriend even if you paid him a million quid."

Higgs snorted. "It's not him we're going to see, guv. It's one of the poor unfortunates who has to work for him."

Higgs pushed his way through a door that had last seen a fresh coat of paint in about 1965. The décor of the room they went into was not in a much better state. From behind a counter at the end of the room, the sergeant in question looked up and glared at them. "Waddyawant, Higgs?" he asked in a voice that didn't even hint of cooperation. Smith pointedly ignored Alex. Alex ignored him right back and let Higgs do the talking.

"I want five minutes with your assistant. Where is he?"

'Satan' shuffled some paperwork. "He's busy. Some of us have to work for a living, not like you bloody prima donnas upstairs." His piggy little eyes revealed his curiosity.

"Well, let him take his break now so we can talk to him," Higgs persisted.

Alex just wanted to wipe the smile off Smith's obnoxious, greasy face. With his fist.

Smith pursed his bloated lips. "He doesn't get breaks, he's too fucking lazy."

Higgs growled like a hungry bulldog, "I'm losing patience, Barney, where is he? Keep me waiting any longer and I might just post *that* picture on the canteen notice board."

Whatever *that* picture was — and Alex really didn't want to know — it had power. Sergeant Smith's face flushed to the shade of an overripe tomato and he looked like he was going to explode at any moment. There was a sulky grunt.

"Room seven. Knock yourself out."

Higgs grinned, brushed past Smith and headed down another dank corridor. Feeling rebellious, Alex winked at the loathsome obstacle as he followed Higgs and choked back a laugh at the apoplectic "Fuck off, fag!" he got in return. Alex had been lucky in his career not to come across too much homophobia, but Barney Smith did his single-handed best to insure the bigotry quota was maintained. If there were any justice in the world then the repulsive man would have a coronary before they got back.

Room seven had a heavy iron door with a small grill in it. "No wonder it's known as the dungeon, Sarge, it certainly looks the part." Alex shivered at the thought that anyone was forced to work in such an unpleasant environment.

Higgs grabbed the rusty handle and pulled on it, only to find that the door was stuck. "Christ, that bastard. Someone should have fired his arse years ago." He put all his weight into shifting the handle then winced at the creaking hinges as he pushed his way into the room with Alex close behind.

Alex shivered at the chill. It was hard to see much with the only light coming from a single bare bulb swinging from a cord above their heads. "It smells rank in here, Higgs, I think there's something growing on the wall too. Nobody should be working in here." From the back of the room somewhere, behind racks of metal shelving piled with dusty boxes, came the sounds of brushing and the flash of a head torch.

Higgs called out a hello and the sounds paused. Footsteps echoed in the hollow concrete space as the owner of the broom strolled over and faced them down, hands on his hips.

"What now, you fucking sadist?"

That wasn't quite the opening remark Alex was expecting. Blinded by the head torch on the speaker's head, which shone directly at his face, Alex held a hand up to his eyes and squinted.

"Good to know that his people skills are so well honed,

Higgs."

Higgs sighed. "Detective Trethuan, I'd like you to meet *Inspector* Alex Courtney."

"Oh, sorry, sir — I don't get many visitors down here." The voice that responded was deep and soft, if a little defensive and not particularly repentant.

Alex shook his head. "Really? You surprise me. Switch that fucking torch off and come over here where we can see you."

The owner of the voice did as he had been asked and approached obediently.

"Name?" Alex still couldn't see anything — lots of little round glowing spots floated in front of his eyes.

"Trethuan, Sir. D.C. Conor Trethuan." The young detective stood up a bit straighter.

Alex could just about make out that he was wearing filthy shapeless overalls, gauntlets and a cap. It was impossible to tell what he looked like in the dim light. Alex hissed in frustration. "Get yourself cleaned up and report to my office in an hour. Higgs — tell him where it is." He spun on his heel. "Oh, and if Sergeant Smith gives you any grief, just mention that you know about *the picture*."

Alex headed back to the stairs intending to give Sergeant Satan a piece of his mind on the way past. It was absolutely disgraceful that Detective Trethuan had been made to work in such conditions and there was bound to be some kind of health and safety legislation against barring the door from the outside. Alex resolved that even if the detective proved not to be suitable for the team, he would endeavor to find him an alternative post. Sergeant Smith had conveniently made himself scarce and Alex wasn't surprised, though he was a little disappointed. The man was a bully and a coward, there was no way he was going to be around to face up to a direct confrontation with Alex, no matter what he thought of him.

Alex returned to his office and settled down to clearing the backlog of email, official memos, voicemails and junk mail that had accumulated in precarious piles on his desk and in the scarily overstuffed inbox on his computer. He managed to maintain his focus even though he was eager to see if Conor Trethuan had the right look and attitude to take part in his plan. He didn't want to get his hopes up, though — what were the chances that Conor would fulfill all the criteria Alex was looking for? Higgs had seemed pretty convinced and Alex trusted his sergeant, but although Higgs had many and varied talents, he was not known for his skill in spotting hot young men.

Exactly an hour later there was a firm knock at his door. As the door swung open, Alex looked up from his Mount Everest of paper, noting that his visitor was prompt. His heart stopped and his mouth went dry. He clenched his jaw to stop it from dropping. Detective Trethuan wasn't just good-looking, he was beautiful. Drop dead fucking gorgeous. Maybe a shade over six feet, he was slim but not skinny. Hair that bordered on black was pulled back in a short tail, but a strand had escaped the ties and fell across a sculpted cheekbone. Eyes the color of emeralds glinted from beneath long dark lashes. Soft lips promised…

Alex shook himself out of a semi-dream state. Something stopped the young man in front of him from looking feminine, but he wasn't sure what it was. Maybe the pale skin shaded with stubble? The young detective was wearing faded jeans that hugged him nicely in all the right places, held up by a tanned leather belt. His shirt was light blue cotton, the sleeves rolled up to the elbows. Alex caught himself imagining what it would be like to slip that belt from its loops, wrap it around Detective Trethuan's wrists and do things that would make him beg for mercy. He hoped that none of what he was thinking was reflected on his face.

Alex took a deep breath and thanked every deity he could think of that he was sitting behind a desk. His cock had experienced a miraculous renaissance and was hard as iron, his balls hot and tight. He clutched his pen and tried to stop his hands shaking. Fuck, he didn't remember anyone ever having this effect on him before. His body was happily out of control and he didn't think his predicament was likely to change until the young man standing nervously in front of him left the room.

Drawing on all his training, he managed not to hyperventilate and finally remembered how to ask a question. "How old are you, Conor?" As questions went it wasn't going to win him any prizes, but it was a start.

"Twenty-three, sir." Christ, the boy had such a soft, sensual voice. *He could easily pass for nineteen or twenty*, thought Alex, feeling ancient at twenty-nine.

"And what exactly are you doing working for Satan?" Alex had read Conor's file, he already knew the answer to that one but wanted to hear how Conor told the story.

Conor looked at a spot somewhere on the floor in front of Alex's desk. "I'm sure you've read my file, sir."

"Indeed. Two commendations for bravery—injured in the line of duty six months ago whilst undercover with the narcotics division—sent here to recuperate. But that doesn't answer my question. I don't imagine you were originally allocated to sweeping out the basement because of a dodgy knee." He waited expectantly.

Conor didn't look up.

"I reported a senior officer for harassment." Conor lifted his head and made eye contact. "He proved to have friends in high places and I ended up in the basement." Alex smiled inside when Conor didn't look away. The young detective was prepared to defend himself if he had to, but there was no aggression in his look, just resignation. Alex wondered how many times Conor had put up with harassment and bullying. He didn't seem like the type to make a complaint for no good reason.

Alex needlessly examined the report in front of him, even though it could have been written in Swahili for all he knew. It must have taken huge courage to stick with the posting Conor had been punished with. It would have been disguised as something else, of course, but Conor had to know that he'd been shafted. He was either stubbornly brave or masochistically stupid. He hadn't given up. He could have walked away from the job, but he hadn't. Alex was impressed and that wasn't something that happened often.

Conor was physically perfect for the role Alex needed him to play, he also had all the qualities Alex looked for in a young officer. He was resilient, brave and quietly confident. Alex suspected he was probably quite reserved. For a young officer he'd built up experience that could have brought arrogance with it, but there was no trace of that kind of attitude.

Alex admitted to himself that he'd made up his mind about thirty seconds after Conor had walked into his office – the young detective was perfect bait for a murderer. Now all Alex had to do was to sell the job to him. He'd save the details for later. All in good time.

Alex steepled his fingers and spoke, "Well, Detective Trethuan, how would you like to swap one bastard of a boss for another? I have a spot on my team that I'd like to offer you."

Something that looked suspiciously like hope shone in Conor's eyes and Alex knew immediately that he wouldn't have to work too hard on convincing Conor to join him.

"Will you lock me in the cellar, sir?"

Alex smirked. "Not unless you misbehave. I don't tolerate less than one hundred percent effort. You'll work harder for me than you ever have for anyone else, and I don't run my department by bloody committee – you do what I say, when I say it. If you have a problem with that you can leave now."

Conor shuffled his feet and Alex held his breath, willing Conor to stay where he was.

"I... Are you sure you want me, sir? You don't really know me."

Conor's hands were clenched into fists at his sides.

"I want you." *Shit, that sounded bad!* Alex gave himself a mental slap. "I think you'll fit in well with my team. So, do you think you'd like to work for me?"

Conor smiled and Alex knew that he would be dreaming about that single look when he went to sleep that night. Pleasure lit Conor's face and smoothed the worry lines from his forehead. He was breathtaking.

"It's a step up from the last three months, so yes, sir, I would. Thank you. When do I start?"

"Immediately. Do you know where the incident room is?"

Conor nodded.

"I'll ring down and let Sergeant Higgs know that you are on your way. He'll settle you in and I'll deal with transfer administration. There won't be any problems with that once I've had a little chat with the HR department. In fact, I see an internal investigation in Barney Smith's future."

"I'm not really dressed for the office, sir. I was expecting to go home straight from the basement." Conor gestured at his casual jeans.

Alex thought jeans should be made mandatory when they looked as good as they did on Conor, clinging to his slender thighs with some tenacity considering how low they rode on his hips.

"It's fine for today. How you're dressed won't affect your ability to get up to speed with the case." Alex risked standing and leaned across his desk to shake Conor's hand. "Welcome to the team." Maybe he extended the handshake a little too long, but Conor's light grip was warm. Alex didn't want to let go. Conor gave him a mildly curious look but didn't pull away. If anything his eyes seemed to spark at the lingering touch. *Christ, now I'm imagining things.* As Conor turned to leave there was definitely the quirk of a smile on his lips and Alex fancied that it wasn't a smile of gratitude. "There was something there," he muttered at the closed door, willing it to be true. "Definitely something."

Chapter Two

Conor pulled Inspector Courtney's office door softly closed behind him and took a slow, deep breath. He limped a couple of paces then stopped and leaned against the corridor wall. It felt deliciously cool through his shirt, though he couldn't understand why he was so hot—his skin burned feverishly. Reflexively, he bent his left leg up to take the pressure off his knee, which ached sporadically and had chosen that moment to cause him not insignificant pain. It was probably owing to the tension in his muscles. He forced himself to relax. After months of recuperation and physical therapy, he still walked like an old man some days. His grandparents would probably have said it was something to do with barometric pressure. Conor just found it bloody frustrating.

Stopping to rest gave him a much needed chance to gather his scattered thoughts, which he was grateful for. It was almost worth the pain, though the throbbing ache was subsiding rapidly. Conor felt overwhelmed by the conflicting emotions that swamped him. There was an immense sense of relief that he would no longer have to deal with the bigoted, bullying Sergeant Satan every day, excitement at the prospect of joining a respected investigative team and working on a high-profile case, but overshadowing all of that was nervous anticipation at the thought of being in close proximity to Alex Courtney. The inspector's icy blue eyes had seemed to bore into the depths of his soul. In a few short minutes Conor felt like he'd been subjected to some kind of test—one he had apparently passed. He shivered. Alex Courtney exuded power and control with frightening intensity and, somewhere deep inside, Conor recognized a burgeoning need to experience that control at first hand.

"Christ, what's wrong with me?" he muttered to himself. He'd never felt this way before, such an instant, deep attraction—and it scared him. "Pull yourself together, you idiot. He's your new boss, not some random piece of eye candy." He cast a nervous glance down the corridor. It wouldn't do his reputation any good to be caught talking to himself. The inspector had told him to head down to the team's office and start familiarizing himself with the current case, so that's what he would do. Conor pushed away from the wall, tested his knee gingerly and headed for the stairs. There would be plenty of time to daydream about Alex Courtney when he got home that evening.

To Conor's relief, Sergeant Higgs was looking out for him when he got downstairs. He had been a little worried about barging in on an investigation he knew little about and a team of men he'd never met.

"The guv'nor rang to say you were on your way. I understand congratulations are in order?" Higgs seemed friendly and approachable so Conor smiled and nodded. Alex had made the effort to insure he was taken care of. Despite his abrupt demeanor, his new boss was more thoughtful than he looked. "Is Inspector Courtney always so unconventional?" he asked the sergeant.

Higgs raised a bushy eyebrow. "What do you mean?"

"Well, isn't there an official recruitment process he should be following? I'm not sure that HR will approve of his methods."

Higgs gave a throaty chuckle. "The boss had very particular requirements for this role son, I don't think we could have found anyone more suited to joining the team. Oh, and I wouldn't mention HR to the boss, he thinks it stands for Harridans and Rottweilers, which, let's face it, are good descriptions for most of the women that work in that department. Come on, our digs are just down here.

Nothing special but it's good enough for us. I've even wiped the coffee stains off a desk for you."

Conor was nervous, he'd never been comfortable meeting new people—he had a tendency to get tongue-tied and awkward—but the sergeant's lighthearted banter put him more at ease. If Higgs was typical of the detectives he would be working with, Conor thought he'd be fine. The team's office was situated at the end of a long corridor painted in the kind of institutional gray that suited battleships and not a lot else. Conor wondered idly if anyone had ever considered how a coat of sunny yellow or a nice peaceful shade of green might boost morale. Probably not. He realized that Higgs was talking and tuned in to what he was saying.

"Now don't worry about this lot. They can be a bit brusque, but they work really hard. Don't tell them I said that, though—don't want them getting too pleased with themselves. Their heads get swollen enough every time we close a case. We're an effective team, but another pair of hands is going to come in very useful on this investigation, it's a complete bastard. Enough to drive us all to drink."

They stepped inside the office and four men immediately looked in Conor's direction, their expressions full of naked curiosity. Conor felt his face heat. It got worse when two of the men nodded knowingly and the others laughed. "All becomes clear, Sarge. Very pretty."

"Are you sure he's a detective?"

"Is he old enough to shave yet?"

The comments flew until Higgs cleared his throat. "Shut it, you lot, you'll scare him away. This is D.C. Conor Trethuan, our latest acquisition, and yes, he is over fucking eighteen!"

Conor had no idea what was going on. He'd started with new teams before and never been subjected to quite so much scrutiny. He'd expected some teasing, but these guys seemed fascinated by his looks. It was weird.

Individual introductions followed and all four men were gruffly welcoming if somewhat fixated on his face.

Naturally shy, Conor appreciated their quiet acceptance though he couldn't help but wonder about the amount of time spent looking him up and down. He wasn't wearing a tie—perhaps that was it. Or maybe there was a smudge on his shirt that he hadn't noticed. Perhaps it was the jeans—he should ask Higgs to explain why he wasn't more formally dressed. Nobody had said anything about the dress code, but maybe there was some unwritten rule he needed to discover. He could well imagine a man like Alex Courtney having rules...

And now his mind was wandering into dangerous territory again. The last thing he needed was a hard-on in a room full of men who seemed to be examining him a little too closely for comfort.

The team returned to their various tasks, though Conor still caught the occasional surreptitious glance in his direction. He debated asking Sergeant Higgs if it was some kind of hazing ritual to make the new guy feel uncomfortable, but Higgs broke into his reverie by starting to bring him up to date with the Rasputin case.

"Some stupid bloody journalist decided to sensationalize this horror story after a witness reported seeing a figure wearing a floppy hood or cowl at the scene of one of the murders." Higgs snorted in annoyance. "It could mean absolutely nothing—every kid under twenty wears a hoodie these days. But you know what those hacks are like, they couldn't give a toss about the investigation, they just want a nice juicy story to fill their pages and scare the crap out of their readers."

Conor nodded in sympathy, "It is rather melodramatic. The killer probably loves it."

"Exactly." Higgs bustled around, collecting piles of paper and folders in a multitude of colors. "They've turned a psycho into a media star—when we catch him he'll probably end up writing a book and appearing on fucking breakfast TV."

Conor noted that Higgs used the word 'when' and not 'if'.

That was a state of mind that came automatically to good detectives.

"Right, I'll give you the potted background to the case. It's been six months since the first body was found, dumped in an alley behind an abandoned factory. The corpse had been stabbed and slashed just like the ones that have come along since. I have to say that these have been the longest six months of my life, and that goes for all of us. The only solid links we've found between the victims are that they were all gay and that at one time or another they had all visited The Black Orchid nightclub. That didn't take a great deal of detective work, but we've yet to find anything else of importance that connects all four victims." Higgs shrugged. "Sure there have been occasional coincidences putting two of them together—a shared dentist, a recent visit to the cinema, an ex college roommate who was a friend of a friend of a friend. The list goes on but it's all trivia. Nothing significant and nothing that solidly links all four together. Nothing that helps us understand why they were picked out for such gruesome deaths."

"Perhaps there isn't a link to find," Conor said.

"Maybe, but I hope to God there is. As you can probably imagine, paranoia and fear are spreading through the gay community. Accusations are flying in all directions and anyone with an opinion and a platform to voice it from is doing so. I don't think I've ever witnessed such a spectacular amount of arse-covering in my entire career and I know it drives the boss to distraction."

"The inspector looks tired. Understandably."

Higgs nodded. "He is. We all are. The media jump on every new case with a ravenous appetite for the 'scandal of police ineffectiveness' and the boss hates that the team are bearing the brunt of the vitriol. You've probably heard or read all the comments— We don't care. We're going through the motions. We are all bigoted, idle incompetents who should be directing traffic. The story's rarely out of the papers. The ignorance hurts, but the boss knows that every member of this team is working his butt off to try to get a result."

Conor frowned. "I've never been on such a high profile case before. You can shrug off the comments, but it must affect everyone when they're trying so hard."

"Between you and me, son, it does. Okay, somewhere in here you've got press clippings, witness statements, scene of crime photos, about three thousand goddamn memos, letters from nutters claiming to be the killer... The usual. You get started on this lot while I sort out your computer access. I know you're already on the system, but you won't be able to get into the specific case information data. I'll have to dig a geek out of IT for that, but they are fairly bribable. There's not much they won't do for a couple of chocolate digestives."

Conor chuckled. "Well there's plenty here for me to be getting on with."

"Knock yourself out, son. You've got quite a bit of catching up to do. Take some time to look at the incident board as well. Oh, and help yourself in the kitchen." He pointed at a corner where a large kettle surrounded by mugs sat on a work surface. There were a few cupboards and a creaky-looking microwave as well as a fridge. "I take my tea strong with two sugars."

"Was that a hint, Sarge?"

Higgs winked, "Very intuitive, son, you're obviously a fine detective."

Conor got up and headed for the kettle. "Anyone else for a drink?" That got him a chorus of grateful requests. He smiled to himself — some things never changed wherever you went. In a British police station, the junior team member made the tea. It was the law.

Time slipped by quickly as Conor immersed himself in the piles of material Higgs had given him. Four murders had generated an immense amount of information, most of which was little better than useless, but he had to read every word. He didn't want to miss anything and look like an idiot if he was asked a question later.

By mid afternoon Higgs had worked a minor miracle and Conor had the computer access he needed. As a result his workload was supplemented by thousands of computer files. After four deaths, it was worrying that no one had yet seen anything significant. Witness statements were vague at best. There had been glimpses of a man running, a hooded figure in the dark, but little else. Rasputin was clever and careful, a nasty combination.

Afternoon became evening and Conor's new colleagues drifted away one by one. He barely acknowledged their friendly comments as they departed. Eventually he found himself alone with several stacks of paperwork still to go through. He was tired, but wanted to keep at it for a while yet—it was important to him to be as informed as possible so that he could make a useful contribution to the investigation. He kneaded the back of his neck, trying to alleviate the tension that had crept into his muscles as he read. He winced as a particularly solid knot proved tender beneath his thumbs. He dug in a little deeper, enjoying the pain because he knew it was doing some good. He tilted his head from side to side and grimaced at the popping noises that accompanied the movement. He didn't notice the office door swing open, or realize that anyone had come into the room, until Alex spoke.

"Still here?"

Conor nearly jumped out of his skin. "Holy crap!" His heart pounded and his pulse raced. The case must have spooked him more than he had thought. He rested his head on his arms and groaned with embarrassment at his nervy reaction.

Alex laughed. "Sorry, Conor, I didn't mean to startle you. I think you need a break—in fact I know you do, you look exhausted. Come and grab something to eat with me. You're not going to solve the case on your first day."

It wasn't really a question or suggestion, more a politely phrased order. Conor flushed, knowing that he wasn't capable of saying no. "Okay, sir, that sounds great. I am a bit hungry." He gave himself a mental slap for being such a pathetic idiot in front of his new boss, and stood up.

"You can drop the 'sir', Conor—it's Alex after hours."

Alex smiled and Conor couldn't help but think how handsome he was, if a little scary and intimidating. He almost licked his lips at the thought of what it might feel like to have Alex's strong arms holding him but stopped himself just in time. *Fuck, get a grip! You've only just met him.* His face heated even more and he prayed that Alex couldn't guess what he was thinking about. He wouldn't be at all surprised if the inspector could read minds. Alex certainly had the kind of penetrating stare that suggested he knew exactly what was going on inside Conor's head and he'd embarrassed himself quite enough for one day.

"How are you getting home?" Alex asked as they headed out.

"I've got my bike," Conor answered. "If we're not going far I'll leave it here and come back for it."

"That's fine. The place I have in mind is only five minutes away."

They walked in companionable silence to a small Italian restaurant just around the corner from the station and sat at a table next to the window. The whole place was a cliché, with red and white checked tablecloths, candles in old Chianti bottles coated with solidified drips of wax and laminated menus that had seen better days. The atmosphere was warm and friendly, though, and the whole place smelled of herbs and spices.

A short, rotund man bustled over and greeted Alex like a long-lost member of his family. After effusive introductions that seemed to include most of the staff and half the customers in the restaurant, fresh bread with aromatic olive oil was left to tide them over while their food was prepared. Alex ordered for both of them, watching Conor as he did. The overt act of dominance made Conor smile wryly. He wondered if Alex had expected him to be annoyed. A brief look of satisfaction crossed Alex's face and that gave Conor his answer. Conor dipped a piece of warm bread in oil and held it to his mouth, allowing the slick liquid to spread across his lips. He took a bite then slowly ran his tongue over his lower lip, chasing a stray drop of oil. Alex's eyes widened and a hint of color bloomed on his cheeks. Conor smiled innocently.

I think I have a wolf in sheep's clothing here, Alex thought to himself. *Well, an enthusiastic pup anyway.* He could imagine smearing that oil in all kinds of interesting places. It was a delight to watch Conor eat. He twirled his linguine expertly, complimented the chef politely and smiled shyly at the waitress who couldn't take her eyes off him. He didn't encourage her any more, though, and Alex was secretly pleased about that. He bristled at the sight of other people casting flirtatious looks at Conor. Unfortunately that seemed to happen when anyone noticed him. Conor drew admiring glances from every woman in the place, and jealous ones from the men they were with. Alex wanted to growl at them, make it clear that Conor was not available, and maybe put a paper bag over Conor's head so that everyone would stop lusting after him. Still Conor seemed comfortable in his company and was attentive. He wasn't distracted by any of the attention — in fact he seemed completely oblivious to it.

An hour, and a pleasantly full stomach, later Alex decided it was time to let his latest recruit know what he was really in for. Alex wasn't looking forward to confessing, but it had to be done. Both he and Conor had stuck to mineral water with their meals so he couldn't take advantage of senses dulled by alcohol, which might have made things easier. Now they sat with tiny cups of rich, dark espresso in front of them and there were no more excuses or distractions. Alex took a deep breath and tried to focus on what he needed to say. Okay maybe there was still a distraction — a beautiful, dark-haired one sitting just across the table. Alex lost his train of thought as he admired the snug fit of Conor's shirt, which effectively demonstrated a nicely tapered torso. How did the man manage to make a simple blue shirt look so fucking sexy? Maybe it was the open collar that displayed his graceful neck, or the rolled up sleeves that revealed smooth, toned forearms? The leather strap of his watch could so easily be a cuff, buckled tightly... *Fuck. Concentrate!* Unfortunately, the disruption to his concentration made him speak more abruptly than he intended. "Conor, why do you think I recruited you to this team?"

A slight, sardonic smile played across Conor's face, but didn't reach his eyes. He looked directly at Alex, and hesitated just for a moment before he spoke with certainty. "I would like to say it's because I'm a good detective, but I imagine it's got more to do with the way I look."

Alex managed not to groan out loud. "How did you know? Did Sergeant Higgs tell you?" Alex really hoped that Conor did not have the kind of ego that bruised easily.

Conor shrugged. "No, sir, nobody said anything specific. But I'm not blind — I've been in the incident room all day, looking at pictures of the victims, all of whom are young, tall and dark-haired. And for a bunch of married blokes, my new colleagues spent a worrying amount of time looking at me — and none of them seemed like closet cases."

"Drop the 'sir'," Alex snapped, feeling vaguely annoyed that Conor was so astute. "Your intuition serves you well. You're partly right, the way you look is important, but I need your professional skills as well. I want you to play a part for a while, an important one, so I hope you're a bloody convincing actor as well as a good detective."

"I don't understand. I guessed you'd use me as bait." Conor gave Alex a curious look.

Alex tapped his fingers on his thigh. "Well, that is the idea, just not quite the whole story. We need to be a bit cleverer than just putting you out there undercover. All the murder victims were in steady relationships. It's one of very few common factors linking them. To some degree they were all into the BDSM scene—either in Dom/sub relationships or just playing the clubs. That's not a strong link, because only one couple were fully immersed in the lifestyle. The others played around the edges to an extent. We need a tempting new couple to entice our killer out into the open, so you, Conor, are going to become my boyfriend."

When Conor's face paled Alex felt ridiculously disappointed and a little hurt. He didn't give Conor a chance to speak. "You'll move in with me tomorrow and to all outside appearances we become an item. Only the team will know the truth."

"And do I get a choice?" Conor seemed to be pressing himself back in his seat, as if he could get farther away from Alex, but there was no escape.

"One day and already questioning my authority? I thought I made myself very clear. I give the orders. You obey them." Alex glared, annoyed with himself more than Conor.

"I think this exceeds the call of duty, don't you?" Conor sounded calm rather than petulant, just stating the truth. "You want me to move out of my home, give up my life?"

Alex was pleased that Conor was prepared to fight his corner. "It is a little out of the ordinary."

"A little! Bloody hell, that has to be this year's biggest understatement," Conor protested.

"So, does that mean you're refusing?" Alex pinned him with an icy glower, daring him to back out. He wasn't being fair. Alex knew he had offered Conor a tempting way out of a horrible situation only to back him into an even dirtier corner, but he was desperate. His chances of finding anyone who fitted the victim profile as well as Conor did were slim to none.

"I… No. I'll do it. Of course I'll do it," Conor acquiesced in a voice barely more than a whisper. "But you should have told me the truth from the start."

Alex felt a small pang of guilt. "You're probably right. I should have been more open. You can back out now and

I won't think any the less of you. I'll make sure you are posted somewhere other than the basement. I don't want you feeling like you're being blackmailed into this." He muttered a silent prayer that Conor wouldn't take up that proposal.

"It's fine, sir. I was just a little shocked by it all. It's a good plan and I want to be a part of it." He sounded apologetic.

"It's a bloody stupid, dangerous plan, but I'm all out of other ideas," Alex responded with a sigh, "We need to do something unexpected and I seriously doubt that anyone would think that two policemen openly admitting to a gay relationship were lying. It's a fairly career-limiting move."

Conor glanced at him shyly from beneath long, dark lashes. "I'm not a very good actor, sir, didn't even do school plays. I only ever did backstage stuff."

"You've done undercover work before—it's all just playing a part really. You'll be fine. Here—" Alex handed Conor a slip of paper. "This is my address. I don't expect to see you at the station tomorrow. Take the day to pack what you need and make arrangements to forward your mail, cancel your papers, that kind of thing. I'll see you at my place at seven tomorrow evening. I'll give you your own key then, I don't have a spare one on me."

Conor glanced at the piece of paper and slipped it into his pocket. "I'll be there." He pushed his chair back and stood up. "Let me make a contribution toward dinner?"

"No, that won't be necessary, this is work. It's going on expenses." Alex waved at the waitress to get the bill. "You go on, I'll be in trouble if I don't stay and chat with Giovanni for a while. I'll see you tomorrow evening."

"Okay. Thanks for dinner. I... I enjoyed your company."

Conor was a little flushed. He looked absolutely adorable. Alex had to turn away before he said something he might regret so he swiveled around to pay the tab and by the time he had finished dealing with the waitress, Conor was gone. Alex sighed. He already felt protective toward the young detective and yet he was asking him to risk his life to catch a killer. This whole charade was going to be much harder than he thought.

An hour or so later, back at his small apartment, Conor surveyed his belongings and tried to decide what he would need to pack. He should have asked more questions. He didn't know whether he'd be staying with Alex for a couple of days, a week or longer. Would he be able to come back for more clothes if he needed them or would that ruin the act they were putting on? Surely they couldn't just behave as if they had been together for any length of time — that story could be too easily overturned. The problem was, he'd been so shocked when Alex told him the plan that questions had not been top of his brain's priority list. Pretending that he liked Alex was not going to be a problem — he was already partly in lust with him so it wouldn't actually be a pretense. Hopefully Alex would just think that he was giving an Oscar-worthy performance.

"Use your head, idiot. Just behave as if you really were moving in with your boyfriend for the first time." He shook his head. If only he had some experience of that to draw on. He slid open the large doors that opened onto his small balcony and wandered out into the cool night air. He leaned against the railings and stared blindly into the dark. He felt so confused and it had nothing to do with the case. He didn't know whether to feel scared, angry or trapped. He decided on a little bit of all three, but overriding everything was the delicious anticipation of being with Alex Courtney. He wasn't scared of luring a killer, he was afraid that he was falling for his boss. He was angry with himself for not remaining detached and aloof. It was just a job after all and the trap was one of his own making. He had allowed himself to hope that he was finally being given a chance to do the job he was good at again. There was no way he was going back to the frigging basement. He wanted to hate the young

31

inspector. He wanted to resent the man's presumption that he would go along with the plan. He didn't, though. What he really wanted to do was to run his hands over every inch of Alex Courtney's hard body. He wanted to tangle his fingers in that scruffy blond hair and light the fire he knew was ready to ignite behind those beautiful eyes.

Conor wondered how he'd managed to get himself so emotionally tangled up. Normally he was quite restrained and too shy to make the first move. The little experience he'd had with other men had not prepared him for anything like this. He'd never lived with anyone else, never even shared a room. He would never dare venture into a gay bar or club on his own. Sometimes his looks could be a real problem. He didn't like the way people hit on him just because he was attractive. There always seemed to be another agenda that had nothing to do with being liked for himself.

Conor gripped the metal railing tightly, letting the cold seep into his hands until they ached. His cock was swollen and hard. He fought the urge to unzip his fly and jack off right there, out in the open. It wasn't fair! He'd put everything into his work only to be abused by someone with more power than him. He'd stuck it out in that bloody basement, putting up with Sergeant Satan's cruelty, in the hope that one day he'd be able to go back to the job he loved. Now he had that chance but was in danger of ruining it because his new boss made him think about doing things that he could probably be arrested for.

A chill gust of wind whipped hair into his eyes. He'd let it down once he'd gotten back home. Perhaps he should get it cut? Leaving it long after his last undercover job had partly been in rebellion against Barney Smith, who had said it made him look like a girl. Cutting it off would have felt like giving in and that wasn't something Conor was good at. There were too many 'perhapses' and 'maybes' in his life at the moment. Alex hadn't asked him to change the way he looked so the long hair would stay for now. Conor sighed and turned back inside. Every fleeting thought of

Alex made his cock jerk. He needed a cold shower. Packing could wait until the morning.

* * * *

Alex arrived home and ejected his cleaning lady with effusive thanks and a large bonus. When he had rung her to say he was having a guest to stay, Agnes had immediately set off for his house and thrown herself into a frenzy of dusting, polishing and bed changing. His home was now not only fit to welcome a new resident, it could probably feature in *Ideal Homes* magazine. He hardly dared touch anything—Agnes had glared every time he went near a newly polished surface or carefully plumped cushion and Agnes was not to be trifled with. Alex grinned. The old lady had looked after him for years and acted more like his mother than an employee. He didn't know what he would do without her and it was worth putting up with the flapping. She had been relentlessly nosy about his mysterious guest too. The endless questions would have served well in the interrogation room at the station. Evasion tactics had been employed and he had managed to pass Conor off as a friend who needed a temporary place to stay. She'd raised a disbelieving eyebrow at that. Agnes was an open-minded old bird and couldn't wait to see him settled down with a *nice young man*. God help Conor when he met her for the first time, he'd be lucky to escape the thumbscrews.

Alex glanced at the clock on his kitchen wall—it was almost eleven. Less than twenty-four hours to wait until Conor arrived and moved in. Alex wasn't sure how he was going to make it through a whole working day before he got to see the young detective again. He couldn't wait to have his new recruit all to himself. Conor was stunning, but it wasn't just his looks that appealed to Alex. He couldn't remember ever being so strongly affected by someone. There was something enigmatic and alluring about the young man that tied his stomach in knots. He didn't even know if Conor was gay. Now that really would be humiliating — he was far too old to be having a crush, particularly on a colleague. His gaydar had never been particularly reliable but he had a good feeling about Conor. Surely he would have been a bit more interested in the pretty waitress at the restaurant if he'd been straight. But then again, perhaps he was just shy. He might already have a girlfriend, or a boyfriend... Alex groaned at that thought. It would be bloody typical for him to find a gorgeous man, fall for him, then discover he was engaged to his childhood sweetheart. He was getting way ahead of himself. He was a detective. He would find out everything he needed to know through subtle and cunning questioning as soon as the opportunity arose. *Subtle and cunning? No chance.* He had a feeling that Conor would respond to Alex's Dom voice and spill his entire life history if Alex ordered it. Oh, that would be so perfect. If Conor turned out to be both gay and submissive then Alex would renounce atheism and start believing that there was a God.

He wandered into the now immaculate bathroom and stripped off his clothes, dropping them into the laundry basket rather than onto the floor as he might usually have done. Attracting Agnes's ire was not something he wanted to do and the woman probably had spy cameras all over the house, checking on how slovenly he was being. He glanced down at his rigid cock in exasperation. He wasn't normally this...excitable. Most days he was so exhausted when he got home that he craved a soft bed and nothing more. Tonight was different — he ached for release. He turned the shower on and waited for the water to heat. It didn't take long. He slid the glass door open and climbed into the cubicle, leaned back against the wall and let the steaming water pound his skin. Soaping himself down did nothing to help the tingling in his groin abate. He could feel the heat emanating from his cock even without touching it. When he closed his eyes all he could see was a pair of beguiling green eyes, sensuous lips

34

and soft dark hair… He let his fingers drift toward his cock and started stroking himself. God, what he wouldn't give to have Conor's fingers wrapped around his rigid shaft rather than his own. He let himself dream of what it would be like to see droplets of water cascading from Conor's shoulders, running in rivulets down his spine toward the promise of an arse that could stop traffic. He imagined pinning that slender body against the tiles, grasping both narrow wrists in one hand and grinding his hips against futile resistance. "Fuck!" he gasped as the results of his release spattered the shower screen. "And wouldn't I just love to," he whispered as he tried to steady his shaking legs enough that he could reach for a towel. Conor Trethuan was dangerous, but Alex was all for a little extreme sport.

Chapter Three

In between stops to glare at the clock, Alex impatiently paced up and down the length of his lounge. He would have sworn blind that the time had read seven o'clock for the last half an hour at least. Maybe he needed to change the battery. He climbed onto the sofa and leaned precariously toward the wall, trying to detect the sound of ticking. It was working fine — the sound was there, rhythmic and even. He clambered off the furniture and took out his frustration on an innocent scatter cushion, beating it into submission. He resumed pacing, scuffing the pile of the hearth rug into a track.

"He's late. Why's he bloody late? Jesus, now I'm talking to myself. I must be losing it." He sat down, then stood up again, smoothing his rumpled clothes. He was wearing his favorite faded jeans, pummeled into softness by countless washes, hems fraying and a dark blue shirt with the sleeves rolled up. He'd chosen the outfit not because he wanted to make an impression on his guest but because its familiarity gave him a measure of comfort and anything that helped calm his nerves was good with him. He just couldn't keep still. His skin itched. He patrolled the room again, his bare feet making no sound on the polished floorboards. He hadn't felt this level of anxiety since he had been a terrified nineteen-year-old on his first date after coming out.

Little by little Alex became aware of a sound coming from outside. It gradually solidified into the roar of a powerful motorbike engine. Alex paused and listened intently, appreciating the throaty rumble as the bike slowed to take the bend at the end of his road. He didn't think any of his neighbors owned such an intimidating machine — *must be a courier service making a delivery or a visitor.* He resisted the temptation to look out of the window to see what model the bike was. He hadn't ridden one himself for a couple of years, but it was impossible to forget the thrill of all that power between your thighs. He chuckled to himself at that thought and glanced at the clock yet again.

The noise from the powerful machine cut out directly in front of his house. A couple of minutes later there was a tentative knock at his front door. He strolled down the hall, his curiosity piqued, and pulled the door open. His timing was perfect. The mysterious bike rider tugged off his shiny black helmet. A tangle of dark waves fell into place around Conor's anxious face. He shook his head like a wet puppy shaking off the rain and the tousled strands gained a bit more semblance of order. His shy smile sent a jolt of arousal straight to Alex's cock.

Alex allowed himself the luxury of examining his visitor from head to toe. Conor's slim frame was wrapped in black leather that molded itself to his body like a second skin. His waist-length jacket zipped diagonally across his chest, a single shiny stud holding the collar closed around his neck. The trousers Conor wore were enough to make Alex's body temperature rise dramatically, hugging every curve with obscene familiarity. Alex wondered how many other people had ever felt jealous of a pair of trousers. The ensemble was completed with a pair of buckled boots that wouldn't have looked out of place in a Hell's Angels' clubhouse.

"Umm. Hi?" Conor's voice was so soft and quiet that Alex had to strain to hear him. "Is it okay to leave the bike out here?" Conor gazed at him nervously.

Alex decided attack was the best form of defense. "You're late" he snapped. "Put it in the garage, the door's not locked and there should be enough space for it next to the car." He couldn't resist asking, "What model is it?"

"It's a Honda Blackbird." Conor was already walking back down the path. Alex had to turn away. The sight of

Conor's leather-clad arse, as he moved fluidly toward his impressive bike, was enough to send Alex's pulse rate through the roof.

Alex waited impatiently in the hall and listened to the sounds of the garage door opening then closing again a few minutes later with a metallic rattle. He had a scant few moments to pull himself together and readjust his stubborn erection to what he hoped was a less obvious position before Conor reappeared at the door, minus his helmet but hefting a backpack. His leather jacket had been unzipped and hung open, revealing a plain black T-shirt that did nothing to temper the inevitable physical reaction that Alex had at the sight of him. Alex gave himself a pat on the back for not moaning out loud as his dick did a happy little dance in his underwear.

Conor pulled the door closed. The click of the latch engaging broke the silence just before it got awkward and Alex repressed a shiver. "You're late," he repeated. He knew he was overreacting but something inside him wanted to keep Conor off balance and acting like a bad-tempered arse was a good way to achieve that. "You can take your bag upstairs. Spare room's the second door on the left at the top of the stairs." Alex resisted the temptation to admire the view as Conor headed up the stairs. One more glimpse of that perfect arse and the subtle shift of muscles beneath soft leather and he thought he might explode. Better to focus on the dinner.

He made his way to the kitchen, wondering what Conor would make of the guest room, which contained absolutely nothing that could be construed as personal. It was functional and comfortable and it wasn't as if Conor was going to be spending much time in there. If this insane plan had any hope of working, they were going to have to get to know each other as quickly as possible. That wasn't going to happen if Conor was hiding away. Alex had every intention of moving him into the master bedroom as soon as possible, though that was going to test his restraint to the limit.

Instinct made Alex look up just as Conor made an entrance. He hadn't made any sound to give away his approach. Stripped of his leathers Conor now wore black jeans and he'd changed the T-shirt for a loose shirt. He'd imitated Alex and gone barefoot — Alex noted every perfect detail. The shirt set off Conor's pale skin perfectly and made it clear that, though Conor's hair was very dark, it wasn't quite black. Conor looked a bit flushed and there was a distinct tremor in his movements as he ran slender fingers through his hair. Alex glared at him. It was the only way he could avoid pasting a soppy smile all over his face.

Conor climbed onto a bar stool and folded his arms onto the kitchen counter. "Why are you so mad? Did I do something wrong?"

Alex scowled harder. "You were late." He stirred the bubbling contents of a pan on the stove.

"I'm sorry. I didn't realize it was that important to be here dead on time." Conor sounded genuinely perplexed. Alex could see the intriguing glint of green beneath thick dark lashes. It was bloody distracting and he was finding it hard to stay mad.

"You don't get it, do you? What we are doing is dangerous... I was worried about you." He muttered the last few words under his breath and studied the contents of the pan intently. He looked up again to catch a slight twitch at the corner of Conor's mouth, but there was no accompanying laughter.

"I really am sorry. I didn't mean to worry you." Conor leaned forward and lightly grasped Alex's arm to emphasize his point. "I promise I won't be late again, or I'll call to let you know where I am." As they touched Alex took a sharp breath and Conor pulled his hand away as if he'd been stung. Electricity arced between them. Alex felt the downy hair on the back of Conor's arm and the smooth, taut skin over tensed muscles. He wanted more than anything to lean forward and touch him again, but Conor had sat back, out of reach and was avoiding eye contact. Alex stared at him with barely concealed lust. If one touch could have that effect Alex could only imagine the fireworks that might result from a more lingering caress.

Alex took a deep breath, straightened a non-existent crease in his shirt and turned the hob off. "Let's eat." As Conor looked on silently, Alex dished up the spaghetti carbonara he had been constructing, gave the bowl of salad a final toss and poured two glasses of sparkling mineral water. He rounded the bar and sat on the stool next to Conor, dragging a bowl of steaming pasta in front of each of them.

"You should be honored – this is my specialty." He forked some lettuce onto a side plate and drizzled it with balsamic vinegar. Conor smiled and his cheeks flushed a little more.

"It smells delicious."

They ate in silence for a while, Alex casting sideways glances at his companion. God how he wanted to touch!

Conor hauled him back to reality. "This really is great. Do you like to cook?" He licked the last little bit of sauce from his fork.

Alex drank in the sight of the fork disappearing between lips that begged to be kissed. "I don't usually bother when it's just me. Too much effort."

Conor shrugged. "I can't even boil an egg properly, so now you've got a great excuse to go all cordon bleu. I promise to be an appreciative taster. Feel free to experiment on me."

Alex looked at him coolly. "Oh, don't worry, I will." He reached out and with the pad of his thumb brushed a fleck of sauce from the corner of Conor's mouth. He let his thumb linger just a fraction too long then he turned abruptly away and hopped off the stool. "Let's watch a movie."

Conor knew that his face had to be the color of ripe tomato. What the hell had made him say that? *Experiment on me.* Jesus, what an idiot. He wished his trousers weren't quite so tight. That look Alex had given him, so...certain – it had sent signals to his groin that his cock happily responded to. His mouth was dry and he took a slightly desperate gulp from his glass of water. The bubbles tickled his throat, making him cough. His lips tingled where Alex had touched him so briefly. He'd been moments away from opening his mouth and suckling on Alex's thumb. "My God, what is wrong with me?" he muttered under his breath. Perhaps he ought to claim a headache and get an early night – that would definitely be the safer option. Conor wasn't that interested in safe and he had a feeling that Alex wouldn't let him escape that easily anyway.

He slipped off his stool a little stiffly, stacked the dirty dishes in the sink then followed Alex into the lounge. Alex was already reclining on the sofa, long legs stretched in front of him, ankles crossed. He looked good in the dark suit he wore to the office but in tight, faded jeans he was spectacular. The dark blue shirt he wore contrasted perfectly with his golden skin and light blond hair. It also made the pale blue of his eyes seem even more distinct. He flicked through channels on the TV using the remote like a weapon, stabbing it at the screen. Conor wondered if his boss was as nervous as he was at that moment. Alex certainly didn't look too bothered by their situation, quite the opposite. From the way he smirked in Conor's direction, he seemed to enjoy Conor's discomfort quite a bit.

Conor hovered in the doorway, trying to decide where to sit. There were two armchairs to choose from or the remaining seats on the sofa where Alex had taken the corner nearest the TV. Conor acknowledged his own cowardice and headed for one of the chairs, but no sooner had his arse hit the cushion than Alex looked across and scowled. "No. Sit here." Alex patted the space next to him. "You have to learn to be comfortable close to me." Conor hesitated a fraction too long and earned another glare. "Come here, Conor. Don't make me come and get you." Alex's tone brooked no dissension. Conor got up and moved across to the sofa, perching uncomfortably on the edge of the seat next to Alex.

"There, that wasn't so hard, was it?" Alex had sarcasm down to a fine art. Before Conor had realized what was happening, Alex grabbed him around the waist and pulled him back so that they were much closer together. When Alex slung an arm around him and pulled Conor's head down to rest against his shoulder, Conor felt like a teenager in the back row of the cinema. His entire body was rigid with tension but he didn't pull away. Alex was warm and smelled really good. He tried to convince himself that resting against him wasn't such a bad place to be.

"Christ, Conor, loosen up. I won't bite." Alex's chuckle was evil. "Well, maybe later." Alex shifted and Conor found himself held tighter. He forced himself to relax and tucked his legs up. Their bodies fitted together neatly and Conor tried to imagine that they really were a couple. Alex was exactly what he had dreamed of in a man so it wasn't too big a leap. He was just worried that he might forget it was all make believe and enjoy himself too much.

For half an hour they sat in front of the TV in silence. Conor had no idea what film they were watching because he couldn't concentrate on the screen. Alex gave the impression that he was engrossed in the movie but Conor was more than happy with the entertainment provided by Alex's muscles shifting beneath him. The light, fresh scent of Alex's hair made him want to run his fingers through the tousled blond strands.

As if Alex had been reading his mind, he started winding tendrils of Conor's hair around his fingers then letting them go. The light tug on his scalp made Conor shiver with pleasure. He loved having his hair pulled or being held in place that way. There was something primitive about it. Something raw and erotic.

"Does this make you uncomfortable?" Alex murmured, though he didn't stop and Conor doubted that anything he might say would make any difference.

"No... I like it." As soon as the words had left Conor's mouth he regretted them. What the hell would Alex think? He wasn't supposed to be enjoying himself.

Alex carried on, pulling a little harder.

"I'm not going to force you do anything you don't want to — but we have to make this real, Conor, and we don't have the luxury of time to get to know each other gradually."

"I know." Conor whispered, feeling the rise and fall of Alex's firm chest. The other man's strength steadied him somehow.

"Then you'll forgive me for this!" With one firm twist Alex pulled Conor down so that Conor lay on his back with his head resting on Alex's lap.

After the initial shock had passed and when his heart had stopped pounding, Conor decided that compliance was his only option. Alex still had fingers tangled in his hair and escape would probably mean losing some of it. He swung his legs up onto the sofa and bent his knees. The couch was long enough to stretch out comfortably but the tilt of his hips helped to disguise the prominent bulge in his jeans.

"Have you had to explain your absence to anyone? Girlfriend?" Alex's question provided a welcome distraction from Conor's aching dick.

"I'm single. Have been for a while. The job — you know what it's like." Conor tilted his head back to see Alex nod.

"How about you, Alex? Have you had to hide a significant other somewhere?" Conor held his breath, praying that there was no one.

"No. The last guy I was with got sick of the long hours and the number of times I stood him up."

Conor chuckled. "You're gay then? Are you out at work?"

"Yes. For years now. Most people couldn't give a toss, though there are still a few bigoted idiots around the place. Barney Smith being the worst of them."

"There certainly are." Conor thought about the time he'd spent in the basement listening to the vitriolic filth spewing from Sergeant Satan's mouth and shuddered.

43

"So... *Does* anyone know you're here?" Alex questioned.

Conor smiled to himself. Alex wasn't going to ask him outright if he was also gay, but it was obvious he wanted to know. "My landlady knows what I do for a living and she's used to me disappearing for weeks on end. She'll keep an eye on Roger for me."

"Boyfriend?" Alex sounded a little sharp.

"Rubber plant." Conor tried and failed to stop himself from grinning. "Not a great substitute for a boyfriend. His conversational skills are somewhat limited." There, he'd given Alex the information he wanted, without being too blatant.

He yelped as his hair was tugged sharply. Alex growled and Conor felt the rumble reverberating the length of his spine.

"I think you need to be punished for that."

"For what?" Conor protested.

"Teasing me. Definitely a punishable offense, especially as I think you knew exactly what you were doing."

Those words sent a thrill of anticipation straight to Conor's rigid cock. Something must have shown on his face because Alex narrowed his eyes speculatively as if he realized that Conor would do nothing to stop him handing out whatever discipline he saw fit. What had first been said in play became truth and Conor's pulse fluttered wildly in his wrist.

Alex brushed one finger down the gap at the top of Conor's shirt until he reached the first button, his short nail scraping skin the whole way. Conor squirmed and whimpered. Alex's touch left a trail of heat that scared him a little.

"Keep still."

Alex was good at giving orders. Conor was happy to obey them. It felt right somehow. His nerves retreated a bit as he accepted that he didn't have to worry about anything, just do as Alex commanded.

Alex undid the first button on Conor's shirt deftly then

continued his journey to the next, then the next. Alex pushed the flimsy fabric aside to expose Conor's chest. Conor tried to breathe slowly and evenly—he didn't want Alex to know just how turned on he was and hyperventilating was unlikely to make a good impression. He'd never been particularly body-conscious, but now he was glad that he was toned and fit. He had a flat belly and narrow hips, his abdominal muscles were clearly defined. Hopefully Alex wasn't into furry men because Conor didn't have a single hair on his chest. If Alex did have any preferences, he wasn't commenting.

Conor forced himself to stay still as Alex traced lines across his body with a finger. Alex pushed the shirt back farther, exposing Conor's nipples, which were already hard with arousal. Conor closed his eyes and bit his lip hard as Alex brushed one palm across his chest.

"Hmm, I think you are enjoying this too much. It's supposed to be punishment. Keep your eyes open. I want you to see what I'm doing to you." Alex's voice was soft but authoritative.

He took one dark bud between his thumb and forefinger and pinched hard. Conor arched helplessly as the lightening of pain and pleasure traveled from his chest to his groin. Alex gave him no time to recover before pinching the other nipple even harder.

Conor gasped. If Alex kept going there was a very high probability that he was going to come and that would be unbelievably humiliating.

Alex was smiling wickedly, clearly enjoying the reaction he was generating. He proceeded to twist and squeeze without mercy. Conor bit his lip so hard he drew blood. His world became sensation, nothing more. Alex wrapped his arms around him. He was very strong and Conor knew that the only way he was getting away was if Alex chose to let him go. Alex stopped pinching and pushed a finger between Conor's parted lips. He couldn't stop himself as he wetted the probing digits, sucking gently. Alex pulled them

45

away with a smirk and applied the wetness to Conor's abused nipples, no longer pinching but rubbing in damp circles.

"Oh God!" Conor wrenched himself free from Alex's hold, threw himself off the sofa and ran for the safety of the upstairs bathroom. He slammed the door behind him, ripped down his jeans and after a single jerk on his aching cock, shot rope after rope of creamy cum across the tub. The violence of his orgasm left him bent at the waist and gasping for air. Aftershocks racked his frame, his muscles spasmed and his body attempted to ejaculate again. He had no control and it felt so incredibly good. He wiped roughly at leaking eyes and tried to regain some composure. Shakily he drew himself upright. He splashed cool water over his face at the sink and cleaned himself up. Tentatively he looked at his reflection. He was flushed, lower lip swollen, his eyes brighter than normal. How the hell had Alex managed to push him over the edge like that without going anywhere near his cock?

"Pull yourself together. You barely know him," he reprimanded his wide-eyed reflection. He rinsed the tub and buttoned his shirt. He couldn't hide in the bathroom—he had to go back downstairs and face Alex, who would know exactly what he had been doing. His face heated. "Fuck, fuck, fuck." There was no anger in his words, just exhausted resignation. Smoothing his disheveled hair he headed back to the lounge. When he got there he leaned against the doorframe and waited for Alex to spot him. The man looked angelic with his blond hair and pretty eyes, but he behaved like a devil—a sexy, dominant, devastatingly attractive devil.

At that thought Conor drew a sharp intake of breath and gave himself away. Alex looked at him and smirked.

"You came back then. Feeling better?"

Conor nodded slowly, waiting for Alex to make a barbed comment about hair triggers or something similar, but the comment never came.

"You look exhausted. Time for bed I think." Alex unfolded himself lazily from the sofa and stretched, the wicked, knowing smile never leaving his face.

Conor swallowed a whimper.

His panic must have shown because Alex chuckled, "I'm sure you'll find the spare room comfortable enough."

Conor's legs nearly gave way with relief. He needed some time alone to process what had happened and work out what he felt for his enigmatic host. Everything would be clearer in the morning. It had to be or he would be about as much use to the investigation as a chocolate fireguard.

Chapter Four

The atmosphere in the car as Conor and Alex drove to work the next day was strained. Well, it was for Conor at least who stared out of the window in silence. The radio played annoying, bouncy pop tunes that made Conor feel like hitting it with a hammer. From the corner of his eye he could see Alex's smug expression. The bastard hummed along to the current saccharine tune and tapped the steering wheel in time to the beat. He looked fresh and rested, a man who had gotten the requisite amount of beauty sleep. In contrast Conor had looked at himself in the bathroom mirror that morning and winced. Dark circles shadowed his eyes and he looked even paler than usual. Unlike his boss, he hadn't slept well.

Conor let his body absorb the calming thrum of the car's engine, closed his eyes and thought back to the previous evening. He'd handled it badly. When the words 'time for bed' had come from Alex's mouth every tiny hair on his body had stood on end. He'd bolted for the spare room like his arse had been on fire — Alex's evil laugh following him all the way up the stairs. There was no lock on the spare room door and he had stood there, staring at the paintwork, heart pounding, for a full five minutes waiting for it to swing open. When it hadn't he'd had to face the fact that beneath the fear, he was disappointed. He'd had an argument with himself about whether to risk a trip to the bathroom and hadn't been able to decide, when he'd opened the bedroom door, whether he'd won or lost.

Alex had stood on the landing outside the guest room sporting the smuggest grin Conor had ever witnessed.

Thankfully he hadn't taken advantage of Conor's shock and had quickly disappeared into his own room. He'd made his point and that had been the last Conor had seen of him. He'd used the bathroom quickly, nervous that Alex might crash in on him, then tiptoed back to his room terrified that he'd be caught wandering around in his underwear. That very scenario had featured in a recurring, and increasingly erotic, dream that had left him breathless, sweating and wide awake. Three hours staring at the ceiling had not made him feel any better, though he did feel like he had made a friend in the small spider that had entertained him by spinning a spectacular web on the lampshade.

A gruff, sexy voice broke into his thoughts, "Hey, dreamer — we're here. Sergeant Higgs will tell you what to get on with today. I'm going shopping so I won't be around for a while." Alex's pale eyes were full of amusement. Conor decided that swearing at his boss two days after joining his unit would be a career-limiting move, however tempting it was. He settled for a curt "Fine, I'll see you later," then climbed out of the car and watched curiously as Alex drove away with a wave. Why the hell would he be going *shopping* of all things?

Once he got into the office, Conor didn't have time to wonder what Alex was up to. Sergeant Higgs was waiting for him, mug of coffee in hand, and he found himself absorbed into the maelstrom of the investigation. Higgs handed him the mug. "This is for you, son, extra strong. You're going to need it."

Conor took it apprehensively and sipped. "Bloody hell, Sarge, you could stand a spoon up in this!"

Guffaws of laughter sounded from across the room.

"Shut it, you lot, haven't you got places to be?" Sarge growled like a pissed off grizzly bear and the team scattered until Conor was left alone with the irascible older man.

"Where am I going then, Sarge?" He was eager to get on with it.

"All the way over there, Mr Trethuan." Higgs pointed at

Conor's desk.

"Oh, but I thought..." Conor sighed.

"You thought you'd be going out and about like the rest of them. Sorry to disappoint you, son."

Higgs crossed the room, picked up a huge pile of files then carried them back over and dumped them on Conor's desk. "I know this is tedious, Conor, but a fresh pair of eyes might find something new. You need to read everything. Twice." Higgs wasn't even slightly apologetic as he thumped down another stack of paperwork. "Look for connections — anything, no matter how small, could be the break we need. You get to answer the phones as well — the rest of us are on house to house for the day. I've routed all the extensions through to your phone and the switchboard knows that you are the only body in the office today." He paused. "And Conor — don't go out. Boss's orders."

Conor sat down heavily in his chair. "You're kidding, right?"

"Nope." Higgs shrugged. "Inspector Courtney left a phone message late last night. Don't know what you did to upset him but you are not to leave the station for any reason."

"Or what?" Conor felt more than a little belligerent.

"Test him and I'm sure you'll find out. He wasn't specific about consequences but as I'm sure you've probably worked out by now, he doesn't appreciate having his orders ignored." Higgs chuckled. "On your head be it. I've done my bit and passed on the message. If you find anything worth telling me about, or take any calls you can't deal with yourself, you can get me on the radio. Okay?"

Conor hid his sigh. It wasn't the sergeant's fault that he was stuck pushing paper and it wouldn't be time wasted. He did need to absorb every detail he could about the case and he wasn't going to do that out pounding pavements.

"Sure, Sarge, have a good day." He even managed to sound cheerful as he spoke. "I'll be fine."

Higgs grabbed his coat and headed out of the door with

a flurry of advice and a threat that if Conor used Higgs' favorite mug or ate all the biscuits he'd be on traffic duty in a uniform before he could blink. Conor knuckled down to work and, despite the fact that he would much rather have been outside in the fresh air, he was soon absorbed in the mass of information.

Apart from a quick bathroom break and a stop to make more drinkable coffee in the same mug Higgs had given him earlier, Conor kept his head down. Just after midday his stomach protested about lack of attention. He put down his pen and flexed cramped fingers. It was definitely time to eat. His favorite sandwich shop was a short walk away and he needed to stretch his legs—the lure of smoked chicken and tomato on crusty granary bread was too much to resist. The food in the staff canteen was edible, barely, but Conor never went in there. He always seemed to end up surrounded by fawning WPCs and didn't know what to say to them. With his head full of gory, unpleasant information he needed a break. He grabbed his jacket and headed for the door.

Less than five minutes later he was back at his desk, seething. He'd gotten as far as the front desk and had been signing himself out of the building when the duty sergeant had given him a mischievous grin. "You're Detective Trethuan, aren't you?"

Conor looked up curiously. "Yes."

"Inspector Courtney left instructions that you are not allowed to leave the building, Detective."

Conor shrugged, "I'm just going out for a sandwich, I'll be back in five minutes."

"He left very *strict* instructions." The sergeant waved over a couple of young constables about to go out on patrol.

"Hey, you two make yourself useful and escort Detective Trethuan here back to the incident room. He's trying to escape."

Amid much chuckling and despite his protests, Conor found himself firmly maneuvered back to the office. He could hear the two constables laughing all the way down the corridor.

* * * *

It was gone two o'clock before Alex put in an appearance. Conor didn't look up from the notes he was scribbling though he was perfectly aware of who had come into the room. He gripped his pen a little tighter and muttered, "I hate you."

Alex didn't even blink. "That should be 'I hate you, *sir*'."

Conor looked up into an infuriating grin.

"You tried to get past the desk sergeant, didn't you?"

Conor couldn't hold back his scowl. "I only wanted to go out for a sandwich. Have you any idea how humiliating it was to be escorted back here by two uniforms...sir?" The 'sir' was definitely an afterthought.

Alex smirked and Conor really, really wanted to hit him.

"Oh, I have quite a good idea, yes. I've had three different people tell me the story, in fits of laughter, between the front door and here."

Conor buried his face in his hands and moaned miserably—he was going to be the laughingstock of the entire station.

"Perhaps that will teach you to follow my orders? Sergeant Higgs did tell you not to go out, didn't he?"

Conor nodded.

"So now you know—disobey me and there will be consequences."

Conor had a feeling that Alex wasn't just talking about work and to his utter horror his cock seemed to like that idea—a lot. He squirmed in his seat and avoided Alex's piercing gaze.

"You're enjoying this, aren't you?" Conor muttered.

"Yep." Alex didn't bother to deny it. "But I'm going to make it up to you. You and I are going out tonight—do you know The Black Orchid?"

"It's a club downtown—mixed crowd, but mainly gay. Good live music if you're into the Goth scene. It's also one of the few links in the case."

Conor was relieved that he'd been diligent in his reading and didn't sound like a complete idiot.

Alex nodded, "Indeed. Get as much background on the place as you can. I'll be back to pick you up later."

With an effort, Conor ignored Alex's brief touch on his shoulder. Alex placed a brown paper bag on the desk next to him then left without another word.

Conor shook his head, his cock ached and he felt a lot warmer than the temperature in the room merited. He opened the bag and pulled out a sandwich and a bottle of juice. Conor couldn't help but smile when he discovered smoked chicken, tomato and granary bread. Alex Courtney might be an utter bastard but he was clearly an excellent detective.

When Alex collected him later Conor felt nothing but relief. His mind buzzed with information and he was desperate to switch off for a while. Alex left him alone with his thoughts on the drive home but as they pulled up at the house he switched off the ignition and turned toward him. "It's intense, isn't it?"

Conor shivered. "I can't get the images out of my head."

"Crime scene pictures?"

He nodded. "This Rasputin is one sick individual."

"So now you know why we are doing all this. I don't want any more dead boys on my hands. We have to catch him before he kills again."

Conor raised an eyebrow at the raw emotion in Alex's voice. The inspector usually came across as icily controlled. This was the first time a little crack in his armor had hinted at vulnerability.

Alex gave him a tight smile. "But first, you get to experience Agnes' cooking."

"Agnes?"

"My guardian angel." Alex grinned and climbed out of

the car.

Conor followed Alex inside. As soon as they got into the hall, Conor breathed in a delicious, savory aroma. He wandered through to the kitchen, following his nose like a hungry bloodhound. In the oven, a casserole bubbled away. Conor licked his lips and wondered how long he would have to wait before he could get his fork into a plateful of deliciousness.

Alex smiled. "Agnes is my housekeeper. She thinks I don't look after myself properly, and I like to perpetuate the myth—she's a much better cook than I am. She's only supposed to clean and do laundry but she loves to cook, so who am I to deprive her of the opportunity?"

"Is there an automatic timer on the oven then, or is she still here?"

"If there is, I don't know how to work it. We have a system—if I know when I'm going to be home and it fits with her hours, I text her and she turns the oven on before she leaves. Most of the time, I can't be accurate enough so she leaves things pre-cooked in the fridge and I just heat them up. She won't be here now but you'll meet her sooner or later. She's desperate to get to know you—she'll find an excuse to be here, just wait and see."

Alex dished up the food and as they ate, Conor relayed everything he had researched on The Black Orchid.

Alex listened and nodded. "Well, we know that all the victims were fairly regular visitors to the club. It's worth a closer look. We've obviously questioned all the staff already and watched hours of CCTV footage but got nothing useful. What we haven't yet done is go in undercover." He stacked their plates in the dishwasher. "I've got a team in place at the venue—all we need to do is look like we fit in, and get noticed."

Conor frowned. "How exactly are we going to achieve that?"

Alex grinned. "Not we. You. I'm a familiar face in the area, and I've been to the club a few times in the past, but you're not known there. I'm going to make sure that you attract a lot of attention tonight. All eyes will be on you. There are clothes for you upstairs on your bed. Go and get ready."

Conor climbed the stairs with some trepidation. Alex had looked just a bit too pleased with himself. He took one look at the clothes laid out on the spare room bed and swallowed back a curse. His instincts had been right.

"You have got to be kidding me!" His outraged exclamation was met by a gleeful chuckle.

Alex had followed him up the stairs and stood in the doorway laughing. "From my shopping trip this morning — you'll look great! Don't you think I've got great taste?"

"Bastard! You can't expect me to go out in public dressed in this get-up? I'm already the laughing stock of the station thanks to your bloody 'no going out' rule — this'll be the final nail in the coffin." Conor was close to hyperventilating.

"Stop grousing and get ready. Pretend you're going to a fancy dress party."

"What the hell as?"

"Oh believe me, you'd fit right in on Hallowe'en at a club I belong to. I'll have to take you there one day."

Conor didn't want to guess at what kind of establishment that might be.

He took refuge in the bathroom and delayed the need to dress with a long, hot shower. He couldn't hide forever, though, and Alex was waiting when he came back to his room. Conor wished he were wearing more than a towel as Alex gave him a wolfish grin. He pushed Alex out of the room and slammed the door in the annoying man's face just to make a point.

Conor dropped the towel and picked up a pair of shorts made of some kind of synthetic black film. Cursing, he wriggled into them — they were skin-tight and left nothing to the imagination. He could just see Alex picking them out in the shop. He could easily have worn his usual underwear. This was Alex's idea of a joke. Next came black vinyl trousers, laced with chains, which sat indecently low on his hips. Conor realized that actually his normal cotton shorts would never have fitted beneath them, they were so tight. The long-sleeved black T-shirt he shrugged on next was very fitted as well and slashed provocatively across the chest. His own buckled biker boots finished off the look.

Conor combed his hair out until it tumbled around his shoulders in shiny waves. He found a stick of black eyeliner on the bed. He picked it up with a sigh and debated whether to scrawl obscene graffiti across Alex's guest room wall or to apply it. His fingers twitched but he settled for self-preservation and applied a smudged line around his eyes. When he dared to look in the mirror he hardly recognized himself.

He was still staring at his reflection in bemusement when the door opened and Alex walked in. "Bloody hell! You look like the poster boy for *Goth Fashion* monthly."

Conor glared at him, "This is...horrible, Alex."

Alex ruffled his hair, "No, it's perfect. You are stunning and every single person at The Black Orchid tonight is going to be looking at you. You'll fit right in there — practically everyone will be dressed head to toe in black."

"How did you even know my sizes?"

"Elementary, my dear Conor — constabulary tailors had your measurements on record from your uniform fitting."

"It's all so...tight!"

Alex licked his lips. "Mmm. It sure is. Now, the finishing touch..."

He produced a strip of black leather from his pocket. It took Conor a few moments to realize what it was and what Alex intended to do with it.

"No! You are not going to make me wear a collar! I'll never be able to show my face at work again." Conor backed up until the wall stopped him.

"Yes, I *am*." Alex leaned in and placed a hand on the wall next to Conor's head. He slid his other hand beneath Conor's hair and gently massaged his neck. Conor closed his eyes and his lip trembled as Alex slid the leather around his throat.

As Alex fastened the buckle he pressed his knee forward, pushing Conor's legs apart. Conor whimpered. There was pressure against his thigh and gentle fingers stroking his neck. He couldn't think straight. Any closer and Alex would feel the erection that was fighting the confines of his trousers. Alex's breath caressed his cheek. Conor tried to turn away but Alex gripped his chin and held him in place. His gasp of shock was cut off as Alex claimed his lips with bruising force.

"Mine."

Conor wondered if he had imagined that word, but as Alex pinned his wrists against the wall he gave in to his feelings and responded to the kiss with equal ferocity. Alex pulled back, still holding him captive, and for a brief moment those icy eyes flamed with desire. Then he turned away and headed for his own room. Breathing heavily Conor slumped against the wall. *Where the hell had that come from?* He fingered the leather around his neck and grimaced. He liked the way it felt a bit too much.

Alex paused just inside his room and listened for any sound that might indicate that Conor was distressed. He couldn't hear ornaments smashing against walls, cursing or even muttering so he decided that it was safe to get in the shower. As soon as he stepped under the spray he relieved his overexcited cock with a few swift strokes, washed and changed quickly with a smile that wouldn't go away. That look of utter shock on Conor's face when he'd kissed him had been delicious. He hadn't been able to stop himself. Conor was a living, breathing temptation that no gay man in his right mind would be able to resist. Alex was completely sane. He knew what he wanted and Conor ticked every box. There was a submissive streak in Conor too, which pushed Alex's buttons in all the right ways. Putting that collar around Conor's slender throat had been intensely erotic, the kiss had been inevitable, and when Conor had responded with such abandon... Well, that had been perfect. Even better, he hadn't tried to remove the collar.

Alex dressed, went downstairs and waited in the hall. His breath caught in his throat as Conor came down the stairs. Fuck, the man was beautiful. He moved with a grace that was completely artless. Alex had seen the double takes at the station from both women and men as they passed Conor in the halls, though Conor never seemed aware of the impact his looks had on others. Alex was used to attention himself, he wasn't exactly Quasimodo—but this was different and he felt a strong urge to protect Conor, something that conflicted with his need to push him into danger.

Alex met Conor's nervous gaze steadily—he'd spooked him enough for one evening. He handed over a hinged bracelet fashioned from smoky gray metal.

"Put this on. It's got a tracking device in it."

Conor took it and clicked the bracelet shut around his left wrist, where it fitted snugly. He twisted the metal around before asking, "How does it undo?"

Alex smirked. "It doesn't. It will have to be cut off, when this is over."

"You could have mentioned that before I put it on." Conor sounded more than a little irritated.

"Why? You would have tried to argue against it and I would have put it on you anyway. This saved time and energy. Though holding you down might have been fun."

Conor blushed and swore under his breath. "If you've finished humiliating me, shall we go?"

* * * *

Alex had borrowed a car that fitted the image they were trying to portray—sleek, sporty but not overly ostentatious. He drove with controlled aggression, precise and focused, his mind firmly on the job ahead. It wouldn't do to put Conor's safety at risk because he was distracted. He parked the car on a side street close to the club and turned to his passenger. "Remember, Conor, everything we do and say from now on is part of the act. You need to behave appropriately. I'm going to be doing things that you won't like, but all the boys that have died were the less dominant partner in their relationships. It's essential that we come across in the same way as they would have done."

A smile played about Conor's lips. "Are you saying that if this was real you wouldn't be such a bastard?"

Alex hesitated before he spoke, "Let's just say that this isn't too much of a stretch for me."

Conor opened his car door. "Me either." He climbed out before Alex could respond.

A prior arrangement with The Black Orchid's doorman meant that they were not delayed in the queue that snaked around the side of the club. Alex grabbed Conor's wrist and pulled him inside. He kept a firm grip, his every move declaring ownership of his boy. When they pushed their way into the busy club lounge Alex was gratified to see every eye turn toward them. What wasn't so palatable was that the looks were aimed at Conor and most spoke of pure, undisguised lust. Before they even reached the bar Alex rebuffed several lewd propositions with good humor and a stance that very clearly said 'You can look but don't touch'.

Conor kept his eyes lowered and pressed close to Alex's side, not making eye contact with anyone. The barman nodded in their direction. "Alex, haven't seen you in here for a while. Who's your new friend?"

"My boyfriend, Conor." He grabbed the back of Conor's neck roughly and pulled him into a deep, aggressive kiss.

The barman chuckled. "You've just incited jealous hatred across the entire room."

Alex grinned and put a possessive arm around Conor's waist. Conor looked at him adoringly from beneath his long, dark lashes. They had set the scene and it was time to work.

Alex chatted and mingled but never let anyone separate him from Conor, who played his part like a pro, acting as if there was nothing else in the world that mattered except the man beside him. They drank iced water and danced a couple of times, behaving like any other couple. It was close to midnight when the band began to play and the crowd's attention turned to the stage.

Conor spoke into Alex's ear to penetrate the noise, "I'm going to the bathroom."

Alex watched intently as Conor wove through the crowd toward the corridor housing the facilities. He knew that several plain-clothes officers were around but he was still incredibly nervous. He sipped his drink and tried to relax. Conor could look after himself.

Five minutes passed and he wasn't so sure anymore. His colleagues would be watching what he did. He didn't have to worry about back-up should he need it. He dashed to the men's room as quickly as possible, shoved open the door and took in the scene. A red glaze filmed his vision. Conor was on his back on the floor, two men held him down while a third was attempting to unzip his fly. Conor struggled desperately but his attackers were big men and they were too strong.

Alex hit one man hard from behind and he went down like a felled tree, head cracking on the tiles. The others reacted slowly, clearly the worse for drink, and Conor managed to get some leverage. He threw them off just as Alex tackled the second man. It was all over in seconds. Two of their undercover colleagues pushed through the door and skidded to a halt just as Conor punched his third attacker, breaking his nose in an explosive spray of scarlet.

"Fuck, you could have left something for us!" One of the detectives bent down and hauled a groaning thug roughly to his feet.

Alex snorted, "My granny could have dealt with these idiots. Take them out the fire exit, I don't want everyone knowing that this place is swarming with cops."

Conor grabbed an empty beer glass from the floor next to one man, filled it with water and threw it into the face of the least conscious of the trio, bringing him round with a soggy curse. As soon as the three men were on their feet and cuffed, they were efficiently escorted away.

Conor leaned over the sink and splashed cold water over his face. Red streams seeped sluggishly toward the plughole.

"Are you okay?" Alex knew he sounded abrupt but his anger was not directed at Conor.

Conor nodded curtly. "It's just a small cut. Can we leave now?"

Alex nodded, "It's late. Just keep up the act for a few more minutes, while we get out of here, okay?"

Alex took hold of Conor's wrist in a tight grip and dragged him roughly out of the bathroom and across the club, drawing curious glances as he went.

"I told you to stay close to me," he said fiercely, making sure he was heard.

"Sorry," Conor whispered, tilting his head so that his hair fell across his face and hid the small cut on his cheek.

They reached the car without any more trouble but it wasn't until they'd driven away that Alex finally relaxed. He cast anxious glances at Conor who was slumped in the passenger seat looking drained, a trickle of blood drying stark against the pale skin of his cheek. Even in the darkness of the car's interior Alex could see the knuckle marks down the side of Conor's face.

Alex didn't speak until they were in the house and the door safely locked behind them.

"Well done. That was a brilliant performance. I'm proud of you, Conor."

Conor collapsed bonelessly onto the sofa, but managed a weak smile. Alex's mobile rang. The voice on the other end of the call rattled off some information. Conor gave him a questioning look.

"It worked. At least I hope it did. We were followed. The bait's been taken." He pulled the curtains closed. "A nondescript white van tracked us back here, to the end of the road. It's gone now."

"Will it be picked up?"

"No. There's an unmarked car following it but we don't have any evidence yet. We have to follow this through unless we hear differently."

Conor nodded. "Good. I need to feel clean. I'm going to take a shower."

Alex gave him some space. It had been an intense evening and he could only imagine how Conor was feeling, especially after the attack in the bathroom. The shower started running and Alex tried to calm his racing thoughts. Now the evening was over he could indulge himself a little. Conor had slipped into his role perfectly, showing no embarrassment at the provocative clothing he was wearing, even though Alex knew he felt differently. The shiny black fabric hugging his perfect arse had drawn covetous looks and sparked possessive instincts in Alex that had lain dormant some time. Seeing him lying on the floor in the club's bathroom with other men leering over him was something Alex never wanted to experience again.

The shower stopped. Alex gave Conor a minute or two then hurried upstairs and pushed open the bathroom door without knocking. Conor had a towel slung carelessly around his hips and was fishing around in a first aid kit that he had retrieved from the bathroom cabinet above the sink.

"Here. Let me." Alex nudged him away. Conor didn't protest at the intrusion. Alex used antiseptic to clean the cut on Conor's face and Steri-strip to close it. He dabbed arnica onto the bruises that darkened Conor's upper arms, where he had been held down.

"There. All better. You're going to have some bruising on your face, though."

Conor shrugged. "It could have been a lot worse. They took me by surprise but at least they didn't glass me."

Alex packed up the kit then took Conor's hand, half expecting to be shaken off. When that didn't happen, he led Conor past the spare room door to the master bedroom. "We have to maintain the illusion now we've got this far. You need to sleep in here from now on. I can sleep on the floor."

Alex left Conor standing there, staring at the bed, and went to clean up. When he returned, Conor was in bed, the duvet pulled up to his bare chest. The towel was neatly folded on the back of a chair. Did that mean Conor was naked beneath the covers? Alex blanked his mind. If he thought about that for too long he'd lose his mind. He went to a drawer and pulled out a pair of pajama bottoms that rarely saw the light of day, then dropped his towel and pulled them on. A night on the floor wouldn't kill him and there were spare blankets in the linen cupboard on the landing.

When he turned around, Conor was watching him intently, fiddling with the metal band around his wrist. Alex's stomach knotted. The bedside lamp cast flickering shadows across Conor's face. He looked so young and defenseless with his cheek cut and bruised. Alex's heart melted and he knew he was lost. Gritting his teeth, he resisted the urge to take advantage of Conor's vulnerability. "Get some rest, Conor, I'll just fetch some bedding. Throw me over a pillow, would you?"

Conor pulled back the covers and gazed at Alex with unblinking eyes. "Please?"

Any resolution that Alex had made disappeared with that single word. He crossed the room, climbed into the offered space and with a trembling hand turned out the light.

Chapter Five

Moonlight filtered through a gap in the bedroom curtains, casting a silvery glow across the bed. Alex plumped his pillows then rolled onto his side and propped himself up on one arm. For a long while he stared at Conor without moving, admiring the way the ethereal illumination lit the planes and hollows of his face. He could hardly believe that he had been invited to share a bed with such a beautiful creature and for a moment he was lost. He should've just settled down and gone to sleep, but that was impossible. He couldn't look and not touch, that would be the height of stupidity and something he would likely regret for the rest of his miserable, celibate life.

Conor gazed up at him with a quizzical look on his face. "Um, Alex?"

Alex took a while to process that he had been asked a question but eventually managed to respond with a barely intelligible, "Uh-huh?"

"Do you need an instruction manual or something?" Conor's eyes were full of gentle humor.

The comment gradually penetrated Alex's malfunctioning brain.

"I'm a man in case you hadn't noticed. It goes against thousands of years of evolutionary conditioning for a man to ever resort to reading instructions."

"Or ask for directions?" Conor grinned.

"Oh believe me, I do not require a map to find my way around your body, but a little exploration might be in order."

Conor's chuckle was cut off before it grew up into a laugh

64

as Alex bent his head and brushed Conor's lips with his own. It was a chaste beginning and much more tentative than Alex needed or wanted. He stroked errant strands of dark hair away from Conor's eyes then kissed him again. This time he ran his tongue along the seam of Conor's lips, pushing gently. To his cock's deep satisfaction, Conor parted for him willingly. Alex flicked his tongue delicately forward, inviting a response. He wasn't disappointed. Conor reached up and grabbed a handful of Alex's hair, pulling him closer. He nipped at Alex's bottom lip, until Alex felt the swell of a small bead of blood, then kissed it away. Long moments passed before he loosened his grip enough for Alex to pull back and take a shaky breath.

"Fuck, Conor, I was trying to be a gentleman!"

"I didn't ask you to be and I don't think that's your natural state, is it?" Conor smiled up at him, a wicked glint in his eye.

Alex snarled, "You're so shy around people, I just assumed you'd be the same in bed."

"You should know better than to make assumptions. Don't pretend to be someone you're not, Alex. You want control? Take it."

Alex didn't need to be told twice. With one smooth motion he yanked back the covers, flipped himself over Conor's body and straddled his thighs.

"Time to play then. You know I was hoping you were naked under those covers and you've disappointed me."

Conor looked down at his cotton boxer briefs and blinked, "I didn't want to frighten you off, and besides, you have something on."

Alex's thin pajama bottoms were tented by his straining erection and felt ready to split. Conor reached up and put his hands on Alex's waist, but much as he loved the feeling of Conor's hands on him, Alex shook his head. He grasped Conor's wrists and guided his hands to the rails of the cast iron headboard. "Hold the rails." He waited until Conor had obeyed, admiring the stretch of his lean body, then he hopped off the bed and got rid of his annoying pajamas.

"You should be honored that I put these on for you, I hate the bloody things. I'm surprised they're not full of moth holes it's been that long since I've worn them."

Conor worried at his kiss-swollen bottom lip with his teeth. "I prefer you naked, but thanks for the thought."

"Well, I think you should be in the same state." Alex resumed his position across Conor's thighs and teased the waistband of his boxer briefs. He slid a finger beneath the elastic and along Conor's smooth skin.

"I should have got you another pair like the ones you wore this evening."

Conor twitched beneath him. "That was *not* underwear. That was cling film in disguise."

Alex licked his lips, "Now there's a thought. Just one strip of clear film wrapped around you, pressing your cock and balls down..."

"Pervert!" Conor allowed his hand to stray away from the rails and it was forcibly returned.

"Possibly. The best thing about sexy underwear is its removal."

Alex pulled the waistband of Conor's shorts down enough to allow the swollen head of his rigid cock to poke free, then pinned it in place with the stretchy fabric. He rubbed the exposed tip with a finger, gathering a few drops of moisture, chuckling in delight as Conor squirmed and wriggled beneath him. He applied his wet fingertip to one of Conor's hard nipples and leaned forward to run his tongue firmly around the other. He sat back and blew a steady stream of cool air across the damp flesh and Conor moaned, his breath coming in short pants.

Alex kissed the point where Conor's neck and shoulder met, then bit down gently before sucking up a bruise.

"Mm. You taste good. I want my marks all over your body."

Conor groaned but didn't try to stop him. Alex scraped his teeth lightly across Conor's chest until he found a small rosy bud again and nibbled delicately. Conor bucked his hips and Alex rose up on his knees, denying him any friction.

"Oh no you don't. I decide when to give you relief." Alex pinched Conor's nipples simultaneously and elicited an indignant yelp from his captive. Conor let go of the bed rail again and Alex pushed his hand forcefully back.

"No touching! Let go again and I'll tie you to the rails."

Conor's eyes widened but he complied with a moan. "Alex, please..."

Alex ignored him and went back to sampling his chest, teasing each nipple in turn. He licked slowly downwards across taut abdominal muscles until he reached the waistband of Conor's underwear again then stared into his eyes as he slid them down to Conor's knees. He couldn't get them any farther without getting up and he had no intention of moving, but Conor kicked until they flew off the end of the bed.

"Better. You have a beautiful cock." Alex didn't recognize his voice it was so husky with desire. He looked admiringly at several inches of straining velvet clad steel already slick with anticipation and resisted the urge to touch. Instead, he shuffled backwards to get into a better position then kissed the inside of Conor's knee. Slowly he worked his way up one inner thigh planting the lightest kisses in a teasing trail. As he neared the top he gave Conor a wicked smile and began again from the other knee.

Conor whimpered in despair, "How can you be so fucking evil—"

His protest cut off abruptly as Alex mouthed his balls, suckling gently, swirling his tongue around in intricate patterns. He wanted Conor to be in agony and ecstasy. He wanted to make his heart pound and his pulse race. He looked up briefly to check Conor's hands and saw white knuckles, as he gripped the rails as if his life depended on it.

Alex returned to the task in hand—or rather mouth. He

reached the root of Conor's cock with his tongue and began a torturous journey toward the tip, circling and sampling every inch until he could flick the gleaming head. "Mmm." He pulled back and smiled at the panic in Conor's eyes, then without hesitation he took him into his mouth. Bracing his arms either side of Conor's hips he devoured him, savoring the clean salty taste, sucking and tonguing in turn.

Conor twitched and jerked. "Alex! I can't hold on any longer... Pull away." Alex refused with his eyes and took another deep taste. Conor erupted, back arched, head pressed into the pillow, eyes squeezed shut as his body spasmed again and again. Alex swallowed happily as creamy cum spurted into his throat, then he pulled away and gasped as with one brief touch his release came too, splattering his torso and running in slow rivulets down his leg.

Sighing contentedly he collapsed onto his back next to Conor who was looking at him in awe.

"I don't have words to describe what you just did to me. It was unbelievable."

Alex grinned sleepily, "You're welcome. Oh... You can let go of the rails now, unless you'd like me to tie you there for the night?" *Now there's an idea that has potential.*

Conor's face pinked and he blinked rapidly. Alex chuckled as Conor rolled out of bed looking a bit panicked. He soon returned clutching a damp flannel, which he used to wipe the sticky smears from Alex's skin. It was nice to be looked after. When he was done Conor climbed back into bed but lay on the edge as far away from Alex as he could get.

"Come here, Conor," Alex said firmly. When Conor didn't move Alex leaned across and rolled him so that Conor landed half on his chest. "Better. Don't worry, I promise not to get the ropes out tonight."

Conor sighed, relaxed and snuggled against him.

"Just tonight mind." Alex tightened his hold on Conor's warm body. "I'm reserving the option to introduce you to bondage some other time."

Conor pressed against him even harder and murmured, "You're not the only one who can tie a good knot, you know."

Alex moaned, "How the hell am I supposed to get any sleep now?"

Conor didn't answer.

* * * *

When Alex awoke the next morning, he was a jumpy bundle of conflicting emotions. There was sheer joy that Conor was lying beside him, cuddled into the curve of his body, but there was also barely repressed panic that the path they were taking was fraught with so much danger. He was vaguely aware of dreams that had been full of anxiety and shattered images of Conor hurt and bleeding. Conor was too perfect, too beautiful to put at risk. Alex wanted to hide him away and forget the whole stupid plan. His stomach knotted uncomfortably as he pulled Conor close and kissed the top of his head.

Conor stirred, crawling out of sleep with some resistance. It was early and Alex knew the previous evening had been hard on him, even if it had ended well. He grinned, remembering how much fun he'd had tormenting and teasing his make-believe boyfriend. God! He was already thinking of Conor as *his*. He couldn't reject the idea, though, because he really wanted it to be real. He couldn't take back what they had done and even if time travel had been a possibility that was one journey he would never take. No. There was no going back. He only hoped that Conor felt the same way.

Conor turned over to face him and smiled.

"Good morning." He sounded shy and unsure, all his certainty from the previous night gone.

Alex kissed him, long and hard, removing any doubt that things had changed between them.

"Oh!" Conor blinked rapidly and his cheeks flushed pink.

"It really is a good morning!"

Alex smirked, but something about his expression must have given him away because Conor touched his cheek gently, stroking the stubble.

"Stop worrying."

"I'm not." He tried to deny it but it didn't work.

"Yes you are. Don't lie to me, Alex Courtney." Conor slipped a hand beneath the bed covers, grabbed Alex's dick and squeezed it hard enough to demonstrate his position of power.

"Okay, okay! I'm a little concerned. So sue me." Alex's voice was a fraction higher than usual.

The pressure down below eased, but only a fraction.

"I'm good at my job, Alex. You have to let me do it. You took me on for a reason." Conor sounded very sure. "We've made a great start, you can't start doubting yourself now."

Alex thrust into his hand, encouraging him to finish what he'd started.

"I know, but this was my idea, your safety is my responsibility and I never imagined that this would become so personal. I never intended..."

"Intended to what? Last night wasn't entirely one-sided." Conor squeezed and relaxed his grip. "Please tell me you don't regret it?" His pretty green eyes flickered anxiously.

Alex stroked his hair, "Christ no! Don't ever think that."

"Then stop worrying, I'm a big boy. I can look after myself." Conor jerked his hand a few times, applying gentle but insistent pressure.

"Don't stop. Don't... That feels so good." Alex tensed as the slow burn of his orgasm began to build.

Conor kept his movements steady and even, not rushing but not teasing either.

"Fuck, you're good at this." Alex didn't want to humiliate himself by coming too soon, but there was little he could do to stop the glorious sensation building deep inside. He clenched his buttocks in a last desperate attempt to hang on, but it was no use, he came with a shout. "Conor! Yesss..."

The word drew out into a sigh of pleasure.

Conor kept moving his hand until Alex was utterly spent.

Once he'd gotten his breath back, Alex said hopefully, "Seems you can look after me too! Need me to return the favor?"

Conor flushed a darker shade of pink and shook his head. "I was using my other hand at the same time."

* * * *

Alex hadn't set the alarm. They deserved a lie-in after the previous night's operation and he'd told the rest of the team to take their time getting into the station as well. It was Sunday, but murder investigations didn't stop just because detectives liked a day off as much as the rest of the world. Still, Alex was wide awake and his morning had gotten off to a remarkably good start. He was raring to go. He left Conor dozing and grumbling about workaholic bosses and took the first shower before heading downstairs to get breakfast started. Predictably, it wasn't long before a damp-haired Conor was drawn to the aroma of grilling bacon.

"I thought we deserved a proper breakfast for once." Alex shuffled tomatoes and mushrooms around the grill with a pair of metal tongs.

"We do deserve it. Definitely. Smells great. Need coffee." Conor groped for the mug Alex handed him and took a long swallow. "Oh yes!" He sounded practically orgasmic.

Alex laughed and gave the scrambled eggs a stir. "Here, come and make yourself useful and stop these eggs sticking. There's no way I'm chipping egg cement off this pan later."

Conor sauntered over and took the wooden spoon Alex offered him. "Multi-tasking a bit beyond you, then?" He grinned crookedly then yelped as Alex smacked his arse.

"Well, I can cook breakfast and discipline you at the same time, brat, so behave yourself and stir."

"Yes, sir." Conor's tone was cheeky enough to make Alex

want to bend him over and give him a good spanking, but he resisted. He settled for an evil look instead. "How's your face feeling? You've got a nice collection of bruises."

"Not too bad actually." Conor touched his face. "My arms hurt more, where they held me down."

"Much as it pains me to admit it, you getting attacked may have done us a favor. You were already attracting a lot of attention, but that incident will insure that everyone will be talking about us."

"But nobody saw what happened apart from those three idiots and a couple of policemen."

Alex shrugged and started dishing up the food, "Doesn't matter. The story will be all over by now, probably exaggerated and turned into a major drama." He handed over a plate and they sat at the counter. "I meant it when I said you did a good job last night." He hoped the praise didn't sound too grudging. It wasn't meant to be, Alex really was impressed by how well Conor had coped with his role but deep down he wanted to believe that maybe Conor hadn't been acting. Perhaps the enigmatic smile on Conor's face told him all he needed to know.

****

After clearing up the breakfast things, they drove to the station in a companionable silence, parked up and looked at each other. Alex rested his hand on Conor's knee for just a second, but there was more meaning in that single touch than any long speech could have conveyed.

Alex disappeared to his office and Conor joined his colleagues in the incident room. Nobody commented on him being the last to arrive. He settled down at his desk and grimaced at the pile of files that never seemed to get any smaller. He was pretty sure it was some kind of conspiracy that Alex had cooked up with Sergeant Higgs. One that kept him so bogged down in paperwork that he would never have the time to stray.

Every now and again, one of the others would cast a curious glance in his direction but he put it down to the bruises that highlighted his cheekbone and the bandaged cut. They must all have heard about how the previous night's operation had ended, but no one had specifically asked him about it yet. And for the rest of the morning no one did.

He was in the tiny kitchen area making a round of tea when Sergeant Higgs joined him.

"So, Conor, what have you done to the boss?" There was a humorous twinkle in his eye.

Conor dunked tea bags until the brew turned appropriately dark. "What do you mean?" His face heated and he hoped Higgs would put it down to the steam from the kettle.

"He's acting weird."

"Weird how?"

Higgs grinned. "Well, normally he's a complete bastard. He doesn't take any shit from anyone and works us like dogs. Today he's on another planet. I went up to his office earlier and caught him watering the spider plant and humming to himself, for fuck's sake. That's not natural. "

Conor suppressed a laugh at the picture Higgs painted.

"I deny all responsibility." He tried to say it with a straight face but his lips quirked into a smile and gave him away.

Higgs chuckled knowingly and Conor realized that every man on the team would soon assume that the fake relationship between him and Alex wasn't quite the act it was supposed to be. He dished out mugs of tea and avoided eye contact but soon the banter started, along with a barrage of questions about the previous night's operation at The Black Orchid.

Conor answered the questions and took the teasing in good humor. Higgs eventually shooed them all away but Conor felt more like part of the team. It was a good feeling.

"Don't mind them, son, they're excited that the case is moving again."

"I don't mind, Sarge. Last night was a new experience for

me too."

The Sergeant grinned. "I'll bet. You've done undercover work before, though?"

Conor nodded. "Nothing like this, though. I was in the narcotics division."

And glad to be out of that world, though he didn't say so. He changed the subject, "What happened to the van last night? I understand there was an unmarked car on it?"

Higgs snorted. "The idiots lost it, somewhere near Anderson Street. The plates came back as false too. We just have to hope you've caught our killer's eye."

A slow trickle of cold crept the length of Conor's spine. In the raw light of day it was impossible to hide from the stark reality that what they were doing was ridiculously dangerous. Paperwork no longer seemed like such a bad option.

* * * *

Later that afternoon as he cross-referenced a page of notes, Conor straightened in his seat. He picked up the phone and made several calls then checked and rechecked his work. With the amount of paper shuffling that he was doing, he was attracting attention, so he crossed the office to Higgs' desk and tried not to look like an excited schoolboy.

"I think I may have found another link, Sarge."

The sergeant tapped the end of his well-chewed biro against his teeth and gave him a nod. "Don't just stand there then, tell me what you've got."

Conor shuffled his feet—he didn't want to come across as an inexperienced idiot who was jumping to conclusions.

He spoke carefully, "You know that two of the victims had visited the hospital for one reason or another shortly before they were taken?"

Higgs shrugged. "Yeah, we checked into that—one had been to casualty with a friend who came off his mountain bike and broke a wrist. The other had done a charity abseil down the tower block there."

Conor nodded. "That accounts for victims one and four. It turns out that victim three made a delivery to the hospital stores. He drove for a pharmaceutical company part-time and replaced the regular driver for one drop-off."

Higgs sat up straighter. "And the last one?"

Conor hesitated. "It's a bit tenuous... There's a statement in victim two's file that his car broke down in the lane outside the main hospital entrance. It was noted because someone helped him push it down the road a bit so that it wouldn't block the entrance that the ambulances use. Later on in the file there's a statement from his mother where she mentions that his mobile phone hadn't been working. The nearest public phone is in the outpatients' reception and he would have needed to use a phone to call for a tow."

Higgs was on his feet. "It might be nothing, but it merits checking out. I need to get down there with a photo of victim two and ask a few questions. If the poor lad was there, then you've found a solid new link between the victims."

Conor remembered that he should be breathing and let out a sigh of relief. "Can I come with you, Sarge?" he asked hopefully.

Higgs gave him a hard look then shook his head. "You're not allowed out and you know it."

Conor put on his best hurt puppy face. "On my own I'm not, but I'd be with you. You won't let me get into any trouble, will you? Please? It *is* my connection."

He hovered expectantly as Higgs put his coat on.

Higgs relented. "Okay. The boss is going to have my balls for this but you deserve to come along and check it out."

Conor grinned and grabbed his jacket. "Thanks, Sarge!"

Higgs shook his head and shrugged. "Once upon a time I was as keen as you. Of course that was back in the Stone Age...when dinosaurs roamed the earth."

Conor followed the grumbles out of the door with a chuckle.

* * * *

When they got to the hospital, the car park was packed so Higgs left his car in a doctor's reserved space and stuck a laminated police logo on the dashboard. "Don't know why more people don't try this — I could be anyone but I've never been challenged. Comes in very handy."

"Someone told me once that the best policemen are borderline criminals. I think you're a good example, Sarge."

"Cheeky sod. Behave yourself or I'll leave you in the car."

Conor laughed and followed Higgs into the outpatients' waiting room where Higgs managed to get the receptionist's attention by elbowing his way to the front of the queue and shoving his official identification under her nose. Conor thought she looked relieved at having an excuse to escape for a few minutes. She took them into a small office and closed the door firmly.

"Now what can I do for you, gentlemen?"

Higgs pulled out a picture of victim number two. "Could you take a look at this picture and tell us if you recognize him, ma'am?"

"Oh, call me Myrtle, love." Myrtle took the picture and had a good look. "Well, it was a while ago, but yes I do remember him. We're not supposed to let members of the public use our phone, but I felt sorry for him. He looks a bit like my grandson, you see. The public phone in the waiting area was out of order and he asked very politely if he could use my phone because his car had broken down. He didn't have the number of his breakdown company on him, so I looked it up on the Internet. He made the call — he was only on the phone for a minute or so — and then he went back to his car. He was a sweet lad, I hope he's not in any trouble?"

"Not at all, Myrtle. You've been very helpful. I just wish everyone had a memory as good as yours." Higgs shook the blushing receptionist's hand. "Thanks for your time."

Conor and Higgs returned to the station with renewed optimism, though it was tempered with a measure of realism. Higgs gave credit where it was due. "It's a solid lead, son, well done. Of course, now you get to start checking out over fifteen hundred hospital staff! Then there's the patients, their relatives, delivery and trades people..."

Conor suppressed a groan and tried to remember a time when he had thought that becoming a detective would be a glamorous career choice, full of adventure. His memory wasn't that good. This new strand of the investigation was going to generate a huge amount of work and there was still the possibility that it would lead nowhere.

It took hours to arrange the warrants necessary for the team to obtain access to staff records at the hospital and afternoon turned rapidly to evening. Higgs disappeared to brief Alex on the latest developments then returned to the office looking a little pale. He delivered a summons to Conor. "Boss wants to see you in his office. He's already torn me a new one for taking you outside the building, so don't expect a pat on the back."

Conor rolled his eyes. "I'm really sorry, Sarge, it wasn't your fault."

Higgs shrugged. "Oh he knows that, he was just warming up for you."

Conor gulped, straightened his tie and headed up the stairs to the floor where senior officers had their rooms. He knocked on Alex's door and waited uncomfortably until Alex growled, "Get in here."

Conor edged around the door, stood in front of the desk and clasped his hands behind his back to stop them shaking. Alex carried on working for a few minutes and Conor knew it was a deliberate ploy to make him uncomfortable. It was working. When Alex eventually looked up, the expression on his face was as glacial as his eyes.

"You deliberately disobeyed a direct order today, didn't you?"

Conor opted for truthful brevity and simply replied, "Yes, sir." He really wanted to loosen his collar, which suddenly felt as restrictive as the one he'd worn to The Black Orchid.

"And you manipulated the situation so that another officer would be complicit in your actions?"

"Yes, sir." Conor maintained eye contact. He locked his knees and stood straighter.

Alex got up, walked around his desk and stood so that there were just a few inches between them. "So, how do you think you should be disciplined for such blatant insubordination? You've shown a complete lack of respect for my authority and that's something I will not tolerate." He punched out the last three words with force.

God, he's gorgeous when he's angry. Conor was finding it increasingly hard not to smile.

"Well?" Alex glowered and Conor's cock jerked.

"I'm sorry, sir. It won't happen again." Conor didn't even attempt to sound sincere.

"Yes it bloody will," Alex snarled. "For now, the paperwork you've generated should keep you out of trouble, but I swear—if you try to sneak out of here again I will lock you and the paperwork in the cells. Now get out of my sight."

"Yes, sir." Conor escaped before Alex decided he needed more of a tongue lashing and headed back to the incident room. He really hoped that Alex was planning more severe discipline for later that night, because he definitely deserved it. There had to be some advantages to having a boss who was also his lover.

* * * *

They didn't get home until gone ten o'clock. The car ride had been made in silence, the tension between them palpable. Conor tried not to twitch with the anticipation of what Alex might do. The front door had barely closed behind them when he was slammed back against a wall. Alex used his extra three inches of height to good effect, bearing down on Conor's mouth with force. Conor didn't fight him. Alex took possession of his mouth, thrusting his tongue deep. Conor was left in no doubt as to who was in charge and he loved it. Alex's short blond stubble raked his cheek as he ended the kiss. Conor wondered if his knees would give way as Alex glared at him with a look that promised... He wasn't sure exactly but those icy eyes were lit with flames of naked desire.

"Upstairs. Now."

Conor didn't consider anything but obedience. Alex pressed close behind him on the stairs and when they reached the top, Conor turned and backed into their bedroom nervously. Alex slammed the door behind them and whirled to face him.

"Strip." The command snapped across the room.

Conor took a step back. "Fuck off."

Alex closed the distance between them again. "Don't you think you've disobeyed enough of my orders for one day? I said strip. Now do it, or I'll do it for you."

Conor glared back at him but kicked off his shoes and socks, loosened his tie and pulled it off. Next he nervously unbuttoned his pale blue shirt and slid it from his shoulders. His rigid cock burned and he dreaded revealing to Alex that his assertiveness was such a turn-on.

Alex didn't look away from him for a moment. His lips were pressed together in a firm line and a couple of tiny frown lines creased his forehead. Conor undid the button on his waistband with clumsy fingers.

"Get on with it," Alex snapped.

Hurriedly Conor pushed his dark trousers down, stepped out of them then kicked them away. He wore fitted black trunks that sat on his hips and hugged the tops of his thighs snugly. He was fully erect, his cock straining at the clingy fabric, desperate to be freed. His exposed skin tingled. He swallowed, trying to regain some moisture in a mouth gone completely dry.

Alex snarled, "Don't make me tell you again."

Conor sucked in a breath and squirmed out of his trunks. He was completely exposed and vulnerable while Alex was still fully dressed. It felt incredibly erotic. His mild panic did nothing to deflate his erection, which stood stiff and proud from his body.

Alex stepped forward and wrapped strong arms around him. Then there were kisses—on his neck and shoulders, little nips to his lower lip and earlobes. Conor didn't get the opportunity to reciprocate—he let Alex do what he would without protest. Strong hands smoothed the muscles of his back and every stroke against his skin left him longing for more. Alex's touch could easily become an addiction—firm but gentle. Conor felt as though every contact was about Alex establishing a claim on his body.

As Alex pressed against him, Conor felt his lover's erection, hard and determined, against his lower belly. He craved the feeling of skin on skin but Alex was apparently in no hurry to undress. Conor whimpered as his arse was stroked and squeezed. Alex kneaded the taut muscles, then spread and separated the cheeks. Conor gasped and arched, thrusting himself forward into Alex's groin, as a finger scraped across his sensitive entrance.

"You were disobedient today, Conor, and I don't think you've learned your lesson at all."

Conor couldn't think straight while Alex played with his arse. It wasn't fair.

"I..." He moaned as the tip of Alex's finger breached him.

"I wanted to bend you over my desk and spank you this afternoon—that might have got the message home a little better than paperwork, don't you think?"

"You can't..."

"Can't what? Discipline you? Oh, Conor, believe me I can. You are sorely in need of a firm hand."

Conor rose up on his bare toes as Alex gathered his balls in one hand and rolled them.

"Alex! Please! Don't..."

"Don't what? Touch you? Play with you? Punish you?"

"Oh God!" His arse was getting attention again. Couldn't Alex make up his mind? He was touching everywhere.

Stroking, pinching, probing.

"I'm going to spank you, then I'm going to fuck you. You don't come unless I say you can."

Alex spoke as if Conor didn't get any say in what was about to happen.

"No! You can't do that... Oh! Please!" Conor was so confused. He should've been fighting and instead he was just letting Alex get away with behaving like a dictator. The man was infuriating. He was treating Conor's body like his own personal plaything and his fingers were...

"Oh! Don't! Please!"

"Make up your mind Conor. You keep contradicting yourself."

"Bastard!" Conor squirmed as he was speared again. Just the tip of Alex's dry finger was enough to burn. Not to hurt, it didn't hurt...but the heat! He'd never been touched there before.

"You're begging for a spanking, Conor. I want to make your perfect arse all rosy before I take you."

Conor lost control of his world, his body, his mind. He couldn't think. He wanted, no, needed Alex to make all the decisions. He humped shamelessly against Alex's thigh, trying to get some relief, but Alex gripped his biceps and pushed him away, then turned him so Conor's back was pressed against Alex's front. Conor struggled against the arm wrapped around his waist, holding him in place, but then Alex tweaked a nipple and all the fight left him. His dick twitched and strained, his balls were so tight they hurt.

"Please, Alex! I'm going to come!"

"No you're not."

The base of his cock was squeezed and he howled his frustration as he was forced back from the brink. Alex's chuckle was pure evil. Then suddenly they were on the bed, Alex sitting on the edge with Conor flung across his lap, arse in the air. Four slaps in quick succession and his flesh was on fire. He didn't have time to feel mortified, though he knew he should. Alex grabbed him by the waist and hoisted him onto the bed. He sprawled face down, his rigid shaft trapped uncomfortably beneath him.

"Oh that looks so pretty." Alex sounded unbelievably smug. "You're all pink for me. Very inviting."

"You... You..." Conor couldn't think of a suitable name for the man who had turned him into a quivering mass of need.

"No need to thank me."

Conor snarled into a pillow. "Stop talking and fuck me, you bastard!"

"I thought you'd never ask." Alex sat next to him on the bed and patted Conor's sore behind. "Something I need to know first, though. Are you a virgin?"

Conor moaned and rolled onto his back, knowing that his face was probably the same color as his abused backside. "How did you know?" Alex wouldn't have asked the question if he didn't already know the answer.

Alex smirked. "Detective, remember? Not the hardest case to crack."

"Oh God!" Conor squeezed his eyes shut.

"You want this, though?" Alex sounded unusually hesitant. "I would never hurt you."

Conor opened his eyes and summoned up a baleful glare, "Alex, if you don't follow through I'm going to hurt *you*!"

Alex leaned down and kissed him, thoroughly. "Well then, as you ask so nicely..."

Chapter Six

"Oh that does it, you arrogant son of a bitch!"

Conor got hold of Alex's shoulders and flipped him neatly onto his back. Conor knelt across him, pressing down on his upper arms and pinning Alex's hips with his knees.

"I am not some meek little submissive that you can order around. I may technically be a virgin, but I'm not completely innocent."

Oh, his pretty man sounded highly pissed off!

Alex blinked at his captor. "Good to know. Your arse is still mine. You may not be meek, but you *are* a submissive. Though I have to admit that you are a little feistier than the average sub. I think I like it." He leered happily and didn't make any attempt to escape.

Conor scowled at him. "You want my arse, you're going to have to earn it."

Alex chuckled, enjoying the game, "Okay. What do I have to do?" He tugged a lock of Conor's hair. "Rescue you from a tower, maybe? Fight my way through a forest of thorns? Did you prick your finger on a spindle?"

Conor slid his hand between shirt buttons and pinched a nipple, hard.

"Yowch!" Alex squirmed.

"The only prick around here is you! I am not a fairy tale princess!"

"God you're beautiful when you're riled!"

Alex knew he was strong enough to flip their positions again but he enjoyed Conor's show of dominance. It was a show, of course, it wasn't real, and besides Conor was naked and leaning really, really close. There was nothing to dislike about that situation.

"I want your clothes off." Conor sat across Alex's thighs, putting himself in a perfect display position without even realizing what he was doing. His cock stood proud from his body, the tip slick and shiny with pre-cum.

Alex ran his tongue across his lower lip and smiled lazily. "It's kind of difficult to undress with you sitting on me, sweetheart."

Conor scowled and began undoing buttons with fingers that had rediscovered their dexterity. "You are an arrogant, infuriating son of a... Fuck! Why can't they make button holes bigger?"

Alex relaxed and let him have his way for a while. He could bide his time, though his self-control was not unlimited. Conor finally finished with the buttons and pushed the fabric of his shirt away from Alex's chest. Alex thought Conor's green eyes were a little glazed. He hissed as Conor grazed his nipple with the pad of his thumb.

"Sensitive, huh?" Conor took full advantage of Alex's inadvertent revelation and began to tweak and pinch. It felt good. Too good. If his cock could get any harder, Alex had never experienced it before. He absolutely did not want to come until he was buried balls-deep in Conor's arse but he was getting uncomfortably close and he still had his trousers on.

Just when Alex thought he could take it no longer, Conor stopped. Alex whimpered most uncharacteristically but the tiny sound morphed into a moan as Conor unzipped his trousers and knelt up so that he could shove them down, taking Alex's underwear with them. Alex was caught between the sensation of air on his cock, which was celebrating freedom with a jerky little dance, and the delights of a close-up view of Conor's firm, smooth balls. He counted himself lucky that sight and touch were senses that could operate independently of each other. Of course, his vision was unimportant when Conor took a firm hold of his dick and stroked because he could no longer see anything except little dancing stars. He really had to stop this before he embarrassed himself. With a supreme effort, Alex grabbed Conor's arms and wrestled him onto his back. He got a bit tangled up in his trousers on the way and kicked the garments around his ankles off onto the floor.

"Oh, for fuck's sake!" Alex realized that although he'd taken his shoes off earlier, he still wore his socks. He was naked apart from a pair of black, thermal socks and that was not a good look. Why was ravishing a man never quite as straightforward as it was in his dreams?

"Move an inch and I will strap you down." Alex hopped off the bed then dragged off his socks before he settled back between Conor's knees. Conor bit his lip, and was obviously trying hard not to laugh. Alex shimmied up Conor's lean body and dipped down to kiss him. Oh, Conor tasted good. Addictive. Alex reached beneath the pillow and grabbed a condom and lube. He had to keep reminding himself that Conor was a virgin. He would need gentle, careful preparation despite the fact that Alex really wanted to just spear him deep until he screamed.

He put the condom to one side and used some of the lube to slick his fingers. He gripped Conor's thighs, then pushed them apart, exposing the sweet, dark entrance that he sought. He stared into Conor's eyes as he pressed his fingertip against resistant muscle, watching for any sign of discomfort. Conor looked so trusting, so eager... All his previous dominance gone. Alex pressed harder until his invasion was accepted. He stroked the inner walls of Conor's channel—it was warm and smooth, gripping him tenaciously.

Alex added a second finger and Conor's lips parted with a little gasp. Carefully, Alex moved them apart, stretching Conor, making him ready. "Three now." He wasn't asking. Alex had gone well beyond the point of no return. He withdrew, smoothed more slick onto his skin and pushed in again. This time he felt for the little bundle of nerves that would make Conor forget any pain. Yes. Just there. He pressed. Conor gasped and jerked his hips up helping Alex drive deeper inside.

"Please, Alex, take me. Now!" Conor could barely get the words out.

Alex smirked, "Are you sure? You're so tight. I'll try to make sure it doesn't hurt but I can't promise."

"Alex! Stop talking and fuck me! Anyone would think you were the virgin!"

Alex wiggled his fingers, enjoying the teasing. "I give the orders, sunshine, remember?"

Conor banged his head back against the pillow. "I'm not going to beg!"

"Really?" Alex withdrew completely and waited. He didn't have to wait long.

"You bastard!" Conor squirmed delightfully, "Okay! Please... Please fuck me, sir!"

"Sir, hmm... I like that." Alex grabbed another pillow and shoved it beneath Conor's hips, raising his arse a little. The teasing was fun but he was suffering as much as Conor from the delay. He smoothed on a condom and coated it liberally with lube. He hoisted Conor's calves onto his shoulders and pushed his legs back until he was nicely exposed. Conor looked nervous and vulnerable and utterly gorgeous.

"Trust me." Alex pressed the head of his dick against Conor's entrance and paused.

Conor blinked. "I do."

"I'll be gentle, I promise." Alex penetrated him slowly but steadily.

"Fuck gentle!" Conor jerked his hips, dragging Alex deeper. Alex went completely still—he couldn't believe what Conor had done. He was desperate to move but waited until Conor's breathing changed from gasps to panting.

"Fuck me, Alex. Fuck me until I can't think, or see, or..."

The tight constriction he felt took Alex's breath away. He pulled out to his tip then slammed back in to his full length, again and again. The world went away, replaced by sound and sensation. Conor's needy whimpers and his own grunts overlapped. Conor squeezed with his inner muscles and Alex thought he might explode.

He managed to hold back for another thrust. Conor's cock spurted streams of cum onto his belly and chest as he finally lost control with a scream. Alex leaned over him, pushing deep. Heat shot through him and his muscles trembled as he came, the tremors of his release shaking him to the core. Spent, he slipped free of Conor's body and collapsed onto the bed next to him. He disposed of the condom then turned onto his side and slung his arm across Conor's waist. Feelings of jealous possessiveness coursed through him. "You're mine. Do you understand?" He kissed Conor gently. "Mine."

Conor smiled, his eyes glowing with an inner fire. "Yours," he replied softly.

"I didn't hurt you, did I?" Alex murmured. Conor moved in his hold, pushed Alex on to his back and rested his head on Alex's chest. Oh that felt good. The weight. The softness of Conor's hair. The warmth. Conor shifted, snuggling closer.

"A little. You're big." Conor murmured.

"I shouldn't have pushed you so fast." Alex stroked Conor's dark locks.

"You weren't the only one moving this along, Alex. I wanted it just as much as you did. I realize we've only known each other a short while, but this felt so right. It was exactly how I imagined it would be... And I like the ache. I love having a reminder that you were inside me."

Alex thought he might be dreaming. This stunning, responsive man was saying things that made him shiver with pleasure. He'd never met anyone who made him feel this way before. Even better, Conor didn't seem to mind that Alex was dominant in the bedroom—enjoyed it in fact. Alex loved that he wasn't a complete pushover. He'd never been attracted to men who wanted him to make all the running and Conor had proved that he might be submissive but could also demand what he wanted. Alex wondered how much recovery time they'd need before going for another round. He sighed. Conor would be sore and he had to remember his manners. He didn't want to scare his new lover away.

"We should shower, you're all sticky." He smiled as Conor pouted and clung to him. "I know, I know. I don't want to move either, and the idea of being cemented to you in the morning does have some appeal, but I'd really like to spend some time soaping you down."

"Oh God, you're making me hard again!"

"One of the benefits of being twenty-three years old." Alex slid his hand beneath the covers to check the evidence. "It might take me a little longer." Beneath his fingers, Conor's cock was rapidly filling. Alex stroked the velvety skin lightly, "So, can I tempt you out of bed with the promise of hot water and me to scrub your back?"

Conor slid from beneath the covers, grabbed Alex's hand and dragged him along, "Way ahead of you."

Alex soon decided that showering alone was no longer something he had any interest in, not with Conor's lithe body to play with. He turned on the spray in the en suite shower and gave thanks that he'd had the foresight to install a double-width cubicle. It heated quickly and Conor stepped in first. Alex watched for a minute while Conor closed his eyes and allowed the water to sluice through his hair and down his body. Fuck, he was gorgeous. Alex wondered what had motivated Conor to become a policeman rather than the highly paid model he could probably have been but then he realized that Conor would hate parading in front of an audience. He was very shy around most people.

"Are you going to stand there ogling or join me in here?" Conor drew a little smiley face on the steam-covered shower screen. "You promised to scrub my back."

"Well, God forbid I should break a promise." Alex slid the screen closed behind him as he stepped under the water. Conor blinked the water from his long, dark lashes and nibbled on his lower lip.

"Let me wash you first?" Conor asked hesitantly.

Alex nodded. Just the idea of Conor's hands on his body was enough to perk up his flaccid dick. Conor squeezed a dollop of grapefruit-scented gel onto his palm and rubbed his hands together until he had a nice lather. He smoothed the creamy bubbles over Alex's shoulders then down his chest, rubbing them in gently. Alex sucked in his breath when Conor ghosted his fingers across nipples that peaked into hardness.

"So sensitive. I like that." Conor gave him a coy smile, rinsed the soap away then proceeded to lap at each dark bud in turn. Alex resisted the urge to grab a handful of Conor's hair and hold him in place. Each tentative lick sent a bolt of lightning to his groin and he had to lean back against the tiles in case his knees buckled. Sprawling in the bottom of the shower would not be dignified.

Conor went for the shower gel again and this time slid the soap across Alex's belly before moving lower to wash his cock and balls. "Have to be very thorough down here, I hope you don't mind?"

Alex muttered something incoherent as Conor turned him around and rubbed more lather into his back and his arse. A warm trickle of water slid down his crack as his cheeks were parted and ... "Oh holy fuck!" Conor licked around the edge of Alex's hole and pushed the tip of his tongue just inside. Alex slapped his hands against the slick tiles and thrust his arse back shamelessly. He didn't bottom, not for anyone, but he loved the intimate touch of a skilled tongue.

The probing stopped and Alex turned, disappointed. The feeling didn't last when he saw Conor, on his knees, eyeing his cock greedily. He barely had time to lean back against the tiles before Conor took him into the moist heat of his mouth. This time Alex couldn't resist and grabbed two handfuls of hair. He held Conor firmly, pleased when he didn't try to pull away. He was careful not to force him too close, giving him enough leeway to pull off if he wanted to. Conor didn't stop. He held Alex's thighs for balance and sucked hungrily. He licked and swirled his tongue, first tormenting the tip of Alex's shaft, then tonguing his balls and nuzzling at the root. The slow burn of his orgasm started at the base of Alex's skull, accelerated the length of his spine and burst from his cock in a hot spray that Conor swallowed with relish.

Alex took a few shuddering breaths. "That... You... I..."

"You're not making a lot of sense, Alex." Conor clambered to his feet and rubbed at the red patches on his knees. "I hope you have a big hot water tank, because you still haven't scrubbed my back."

"Oh, you brat!" Alex pulled Conor close and gave his arse a couple of firm slaps. Conor was rock hard against his thigh. Alex took a long handled brush from a hook and rubbed some gel into the soft bristles. He spun Conor around and pushed him against the wall. Conor moaned his pleasure as Alex used the brush on his shoulders and his back. His arse got the same treatment, though Alex was gentle because Conor's skin was still a little pink from the slaps and earlier spanking.

"Turn around." Alex had to clear his throat he sounded so gruff. Conor's eyes were wide, his lips parted. Alex took advantage and kissed him hard—those lips needed to be more swollen. So did Conor's sweet, rosy nipples. Alex applied the brush and grinned as Conor squirmed and tried to escape.

"No you don't! Put your hands over your head and hold the shower head."

"No! I..." Conor protested.

"Do as you're told, Conor." Alex commanded and this time he was obeyed. Conor stretched upwards. Alex moved the brush downwards. He rubbed the bristles over Conor's balls then along the length of his straining dick.

"Oh! It prickles, Alex!"

"Do you want me to stop?" Alex kept moving the brush head in little circles.

"Yes! No! I don't, can't..." Meaningless words spilled from Conor's lips. Alex brushed the very tip of Conor's leaking cock and he came with a shout.

Alex dropped the brush and steadied Conor as he swayed. The water was rapidly cooling so he turned off the shower and slid the cubicle door open. "Are you going to fall over if I leave you alone?"

"If I do, it's your fault." Conor grinned. "I'm fine."

Alex shook his head. "You're going to be a handful, aren't you?" He stepped out of the shower into the bathroom and shivered at the change of temperature. Conor followed him. It was a shame to cover up all that glistening wet skin but Alex grabbed a towel and wrapped it around Conor's shoulders, looking after his lover before taking another towel for himself.

"Would you rather I was more compliant?" Conor rubbed at his hair roughly.

"And have no excuses to spank that gorgeous arse? No. I don't think so." Alex smiled as color flushed Conor's cheeks.

"You don't need an excuse." Conor ducked out of the room before Alex could process that comment.

Alex pulled on a robe and moved into the bedroom. Conor was crawling into bed, plumping pillows and straightening the covers as he went. Alex grinned. He hadn't slept with a warm body next to him for a long time. "I'm going to make hot chocolate, do you want some?" Christ, Conor was beautiful when he smiled.

"Please."

Alex was reluctant to leave the bedroom but his stomach growled and the lure of rich chocolate was strong. He took one final look at Conor, trying to imprint an image to take downstairs with him. His long damp hair was fanned on the pillow and his eyes glinted green in the low light. His lips were kiss-swollen and pink. Alex took a step toward the bed then wrenched himself away with a wry chuckle.

Alex padded downstairs to the kitchen and set a pan of

milk on the hob to heat. He found a tray and put a plate of Agnes' home-baked oat and raisin cookies on it. It was all so cozy and domestic and it felt good. Having something else, some*one* else to focus on was a novelty. It had been a long time since Alex had been able to switch off from a case and get some real rest. For the last couple of hours the murder investigation hadn't even entered his mind. He felt a pang of guilt but then brushed the feeling away. He sacrificed enough of himself for his job—he was entitled to some self-indulgence every now and again.

Tiny bubbles appeared in the milk and he turned down the heat before it boiled and burned. He used a combination of dark chocolate powder and solid chocolate that melted slowly into the milk to make the drink. The result was smooth, creamy and gave his tongue an orgasm every time he made it. Alex poured two big mugs then dropped a handful of mini pink marshmallows into the top of each. He picked up the tray and went back upstairs. He'd been away from Conor for all of ten minutes but couldn't wait to see him again. "What a wuss," he muttered as he pushed open the door with a bare foot.

"Talking to yourself?" Conor sat up in bed and gave him a mischievous grin. "Should I be worried?"

Alex put the tray down on the bedside table and handed Conor a mug of chocolate. "Oh you should be worried... about being able to sit down at work tomorrow if you carry on cheeking me."

Conor peered into his mug, "Pink marshmallows! Oh my God, Alex, just wait until I tell Sarge and the others about this!"

"One more word and you'll be back sweeping out the basement," Alex growled.

"You wouldn't!" Conor protested.

"No, I don't suppose I would, but I would send you to work with a butt plug up your arse, strapped into a harness and locked in place."

Conor's eyes widened. "Oh."

Alex grinned. "I think you like that idea."

"No! No, I don't!"

"You do. Just think how it would feel. The pressure inside you all day, so full. You'd be beautifully stretched for me." Alex shucked off his robe, grabbed the plate of cookies and got into bed. He put the plate between them and sipped his chocolate. "Mm. Heaven. Cookie?"

Conor looked at him. "How can you just...? Oh never mind." He took a cookie and munched away, then finished his drink. He leaned across Alex to put his crockery back on the tray then sank down on Alex's chest.

"I'm dropping crumbs on you." Alex finished his own drink and got rid of the mug. He brushed a few stray cookie crumbs from Conor's shoulder and pulled him closer. He wriggled deeper under the covers and reached out to turn off the bedside lamp. Conor murmured something but the sound was muffled and indistinct.

As they both drifted into sleep, Alex realized that he was falling in love with the beautiful, amazing creature in his arms. This was a first for him, and it was terrifying. The thought of losing what he had found made him feel physically ill. He tightened his hold on the warm body pressed against him and closed his eyes. The morning would be soon enough to face reality.

Chapter Seven

Conor woke to the sound of Robbie Williams belting out *Let me Entertain You* on the radio. It added to his general sense of confusion because his alarm clock was an old-fashioned one that just jangled harshly in his ear. He'd never bothered to replace it because no matter how many times he threw it across the room, it never broke. There were a couple of other factors contributing to his general state of mind. Firstly, his arse ached. Not in the way it ached when he'd been sitting on a hard chair for too long but a deep-seated gentle throb that wasn't unpleasant. Secondly, he was lying on his stomach, face turned toward the clock radio that wasn't his and he was pinned down by the weight of someone's arm across his back. He lay still, keeping his breathing steady, and counted to ten. *Oh! Holy hellfire! Alex.*

Everything flooded back and Conor smiled into his pillow.

"Good morning."

Conor turned toward the source of the greeting and found himself folded into a warm embrace.

"How are you feeling?" The low timbre of Alex's voice vibrated through Conor's body. He knew the inquiry didn't concern the general state of his health.

"Let's just say you left an impression." He liked it too, liked being able to feel where Alex had claimed him.

Alex chuckled. "Good. It'll give you something to remember me by today."

Alex felt so solid and safe, Conor half wished they were in jobs where taking a duvet day was allowed. But they weren't and the alarm had already gone off. If they didn't get up soon they were going to be late.

Alex was clearly thinking the same thing because he sighed and loosened his grip. "You happy with coffee here and a bacon roll at the station?"

Conor sat up. "Sure. You want first shower?"

Alex clambered out of bed and stretched. Conor swallowed at the sight. Alex had an amazing body, more heavily muscled than his own and skin that was more golden. Conor had to fight back the urge to touch, lick, taste... Anything.

Alex smirked. "You go first. I'll get the coffee on. The shower has a useful cold setting by the way."

Conor drew his knees up beneath the covers. Alex obviously had X-ray vision and could see the rock-hard erection that Conor was trying to hide.

"You did that on purpose," Conor muttered as Alex covered himself up in a robe.

"Maybe." Alex bent down and kissed him, cupping the back of his neck firmly. "And I really wish I could throw you down and take your gorgeous arse right this minute, but the spectacular sex will have to wait until tonight."

Oh, Alex tasted good. Conor wished the kiss could go on forever but Alex eventually pulled away with a regretful sigh. "We can't allow this to distract us from the job."

"This being...?"

"Us. You and me. Together. Boyfriends for real."

Conor felt all gooey inside. "I know and it won't. Hopefully we'll be even more convincing. A nice tempting target for our psycho."

Alex's eyes clouded. "This whole plan is a fucking stupid idea. Not just stupid — crazy."

Conor slipped out of bed and gave him a hug. "No it isn't. If you hadn't come up with your plan, I might never have met you and that would have been disastrous."

Alex pulled him close, both hands on Conor's bare arse. "Stop talking sense and let me kiss you."

Conor tilted his head back and parted his lips obediently. The kiss that followed was hard, aggressive and all about possession. It made Conor even harder and he knew his erection pressed against Alex's body. He took a gasping breath. "Shower. Coffee. Now."

Alex grinned but let him go and Conor ran for the bathroom.

****

After hastily swallowing cups of extra strong coffee they made it to work for seven o'clock with a couple of minutes to spare. Alex bought the promised bacon sandwiches from the staff canteen then they went their separate ways, Alex to his office and Conor to the incident room. Conor felt strange — he was hiding a big secret from his colleagues. He wondered if they would be able to tell that he and Alex had fucked. Did he look different now that he had lost his virginity? He certainly felt different. He felt warm inside knowing that Alex cared for him. Of course the man was an overprotective, dominant arse but he was also kind, considerate and drop dead gorgeous. As boyfriend material, he was pretty damn near perfect.

Sergeant Higgs wandered in, cursing the weather grumpily and shrugging off his raincoat.

"Morning, Sarge, where's everyone else today?" Conor gestured at the set of empty desks around him.

"Out pounding the pavements around the hospital. The new link you found gave us whole new areas of town to door knock." Sarge hung his coat up on the rickety, old-fashioned stand and headed for the kettle with the purpose of a drowning man sighting land.

Conor chewed on his bacon sandwich, feeling a little guilty that he was sat in the warm, munching away, and his colleagues were out in the cold. "I suppose that doesn't make me Mr Popular. I should be out there helping them."

Higgs was fishing around in a cupboard for his mug.

"This job is not a popularity contest, son. This is a team effort and I can guarantee you that they would all rather be out there getting some exercise than in here, buried in paperwork — which is where you are going to be for the rest of your life if the boss has his way."

"But..." Conor tried to think up a good reason for escaping the office.

"But nothing. I saw the guv'nor on the way in and he told me to handcuff you to your chair if you so much as try to open a window." Higgs poured boiling water into his mug and dropped two tea bags into it. He stabbed at them with a spoon.

"Let me do that, Sarge." Conor rescued the mug of tea, added some milk and extracted the battered tea bags. "If you burst a bag it might tip you over the edge." He handed over the tea with a grin.

Higgs took an enormous, noisy slurp. "Oh thank God! I needed that like you wouldn't believe!"

Conor hurried back to his desk and powered up the computer. "I believe it, Sarge. You look a little frayed around the edges this morning."

Higgs grunted. "Grandkids are staying. Little rug rats only seem to need about two hours' sleep a night."

"Two girls, right?"

"Two-year-old and a four-year-old. Bloody hell, if I could harness all that energy I'd be a rich man and global warming would be a thing of the past."

Conor chuckled. A bit of real life put everything into perspective. The world went on despite the murky darkness they were immersed in.

Higgs crossed to his desk but didn't sit down. Instead he grabbed his chair and wheeled it across next to Conor's. "So today you have the pleasure of this old man's company. We have one thousand, five hundred files to investigate, which brings me no end of joy."

"There's nothing like sharing the love, Sarge."

"True. Which is why you get to go to 'goods inward' and

fetch the trolley of boxes."

"I'm allowed that far?" Conor grinned. "Why the hell doesn't the hospital have computerized files anyway?"

"Still in the process of scanning everything, and we have files for a lot of ex-employees as well. They've come from the archive. We're lucky they had everything we wanted and have never experienced fire or flood damage. Now shift your arse and go fetch."

"Okay, Sarge. I won't be long." Conor headed for the door.

"I'll start setting up a spreadsheet," Higgs called after him.

* * * *

"Why is nothing ever simple?" Conor muttered under his breath as he clutched the mile-long form he'd just filled out in order to be able to claim his delivery. He went to the goods inward desk at the back of the building and queued behind two chattering WPCs. That wasn't a problem to start with but then they spotted him and suddenly he felt like he needed a bodyguard.

"Ooh, Jenny, look, it's the stud muffin from CID! The one I was telling you about."

Her colleague didn't bat an eyelid at the inappropriate remark. "Bloody hell. You weren't exaggerating, were you? Hello, sweetie, no need to be scared, we won't hurt you."

Conor's face heated. Where the fuck was Alex when he needed a knight in shining armor?

"Is it true you bat for the other team?" The WPC didn't wait for an answer. "Bloody typical and so unfair. Still, at least this place finally has some eye candy."

"What has Inspector Courtney got that I haven't?" That was Jenny. Her colleague cackled, "I'd have thought that was obvious, you silly tart!"

When the storeman appeared with parcels for the grinning women, Conor heaved a sigh of relief. He backed up to the counter nervously, convinced he was about to get his arse pinched. "Ladies. Have a nice day."

They wandered off, still gossiping away, and Conor grinned as he caught a parting comment about Alex.

"Wouldn't mind a piece of Alex Courtney either. Scrummy."

"Well, now you've seen the competition you should realize you don't stand a snowball's chance in hell!"

Conor shook his head and turned to the storeman. "Hey, Ern, you should have some boxes of files for me, from the hospital."

Ern was short, rotund and grinned like the proverbial Cheshire moggy. "Those two could eat a bloke for breakfast. I do a good line in body armor if you're interested?"

Conor rolled his eyes. "Thanks, Ern, but I think it was you they had in their sights."

That got a belly laugh and a wink. "I could still give 'em a run for their money. Got your boxes in a cage in the back. Won't be two shakes."

Ern disappeared through a door that Conor presumed took him to the stores. Conor leaned on the counter and thumbed through a creased copy of *The Angling Times* that Ern had left there, presumably to entertain his customers. Conor was immersed in an article about the relative merits of different colored maggots when Ern returned, wheeling a metal storage cage.

What Ern hadn't made clear was that the boxes of files filled the entire cage. Conor felt tired just looking at it. Visions of drowning beneath a sea of paperwork filled his mind. Alex would be pleased. Even with Sarge's help it was going to take weeks of slog to go through everything in the kind of painstaking detail that the case demanded.

"Enjoy," Ern said without sympathy, as he took Conor's form and shoved it into an overflowing cardboard box that was acting as an in-tray.

Conor shrugged. "I get all the glamorous jobs." He put his weight behind the wheeled cage and got it moving.

Once it had gained some momentum it wasn't too difficult to maneuver, though steering was a bit of a challenge. The paintwork suffered a bit between the stores and the incident room, but eventually Conor shoved his unwieldy burden through his office door and staggered to a halt in front of a grinning Higgs.

"I don't know what you're so happy about, Sarge, this is going to take forever!" Conor panted.

"Oh, I'm not so happy about the work, but watching you struggle with that thing was quite entertaining."

"Glad to be of service!" Conor rubbed at his shin where he'd banged into the corner of the metal cage. He unhooked the door and started pulling out the boxes, piling them haphazardly around the desk. He shoved the empty cage into a corner of the office and started sorting everything into some semblance of order. By the time he was satisfied with his box mountain, he was covered in dust and a few stray cobwebs stuck to his forearms where he'd rolled up his shirtsleeves.

"Right, that's done. Give me two minutes to clean up a bit, Sarge, and we can get started."

Sarge grunted. "Try not to get waylaid between here and the men's bathroom. If you see any WPCs, run the other way."

Conor made it to the bathroom safely. He splashed some water over his face and arms and brushed the dust from his clothes as best he could. There were a couple of dark smudges on his pale blue shirt that he couldn't shift but that couldn't be helped and it wasn't as if anyone would be giving him a clothing inspection during the day. Sarge certainly wouldn't care what he looked like as long as the mugs of tea kept coming. He was picking a particularly persistent cobweb out of his hair when the door opened. Conor ignored the sound, leaning forward over the sink to peer into the mirror, checking for spiders. He gasped in shock as he was grabbed from behind and held in a tight embrace.

"How the hell did you manage to get so dirty? You haven't even been here two hours yet." The voice was deep, gruff and sent a thrill of pleasure straight to Conor's cock.

"Alex! Let go of me! Someone might come in." Conor struggled half-heartedly.

"Unlikely. All the beat officers have gone out and most people are actually working rather than loafing around the bathroom."

Conor found himself twisted around until he was face to face with his captor.

"I've been working! That's why I'm so grubby—I've been hauling files."

Alex grinned. "I know. I just called in to the incident room and Sarge sent me here." Alex shifted his hands downwards.

"Stop groping my arse!" Conor said, though he made no attempt to get away.

"Why? I'm enjoying myself."

So was Conor, but he wasn't going to admit to it. Alex sighed and took a step back, "I've told Higgs already, I'm taking you out for lunch. It's time we were seen together in a place that some of our victims visited. I'll be down to collect you at twelve thirty, okay?"

Conor nodded, "Yes, of course...sir." A little thrill of anticipation hit his stomach as Alex headed for the door. Conor acknowledged with a little guilt that the feeling was more about spending time with Alex than it was about working on the case.

Once Conor had gotten back from the bathroom, he and Higgs made a good start on the files—making an initial log and cross-checking names against the national crime database. It was boring, tedious work but they were meticulous, knowing that even the tiniest error or missed clue could delay the investigation for weeks. Apart from a ten-minute break for coffee, they stuck at it diligently until Alex appeared at the door.

"Anything yet?" Alex strolled across the room, picking

his way around piles of files.

Higgs rolled his shoulders, "Nothing interesting. Couple of drunk and disorderly charges, one shoplifter, one ancient case of tax evasion. Nothing that stands out yet."

"Well, I'll have your clerical slave back within the hour. We're going to The Highwayman's Arms."

Higgs grimaced. "You look after my boy then, that place is a meat market."

"Oh don't worry, I won't be letting him out of my sight." Alex sounded very sure of that.

Conor looked from Higgs to Alex with a scowl. "Jesus, you two, I'm a grown man, I do not need either of you mothering me!"

Conor stalked from the room and was almost out of the station when Alex caught up with him. They signed out at the reception desk under the curious gaze of the bespectacled sergeant on duty and left. As soon as they had rounded the corner and were out of sight of the front door of the station, Alex grabbed Conor's wrist and pushed him up against a wall. Then he kissed him. Hard.

Conor gasped and struggled. Alex pushed both Conor's arms back until Conor felt the sharp edges of the bricks digging in and scraping his skin. The kiss was intense, almost overwhelming.

"What the hell, Alex!"

Alex smirked. "Getting you in character, sweetheart. At work you can be as bratty as you like so long as you're prepared to face the consequences. Out here... You're my sweet, submissive, adoring boyfriend."

"I..." Conor managed to get a few brain cells together and realized that Alex was right. "Sorry, sir."

Alex tilted his chin up and kissed him again, a little more gently this time. "Don't forget, Conor, it could be the difference between catching a killer and leaving him free to slaughter some other poor boy."

It was a sobering thought.

"I won't. Do you want to let me go now?"

Alex shrugged. "I like the look of you pinned against the wall, but I did promise to buy you lunch, didn't I?"

"Yes, you did."

Alex relented and let him go. Conor glanced at the grazes on his arms and dismissed them as deserved. He gave himself a mental slap, pushed his sulk at being molly-coddled aside and focused on playing his part. He leaned toward Alex as they walked and by the time they reached The Highwayman's, Alex had slipped a possessive arm around his waist. It felt ridiculously good.

"Remember, act like you're up for an Oscar. You've already proved you can do it." Alex pushed the pub door open and they walked into the gloomy interior of the bar. It was a typical Victorian spit and sawdust establishment that had been tarted up with wall to ceiling mirrors and burgundy leather upholstery. The food was over-priced and the beer was warm but the place was always heaving. It was the most popular gay hangout in the area and had a reputation as the place to go if you were even remotely into the leather scene. Conor had assumed that the lunchtime crowd might be a little tamer than the types that frequented the place after dark. He couldn't have been more wrong and he was very glad that Alex was holding him tightly.

Confident as always, Alex strolled to the bar and straddled a stool. Conor stole a look at the barman from beneath his lashes. The bearded six-footer had a twinkle in his eye and leaned toward Alex, looking far too interested. Conor suppressed the desire to say something sarcastic and fiddled with the gray metal bracelet around his wrist. Alex ordered juice and sandwiches without asking Conor what he wanted, then gave his hand a tug, bringing him to stand between his knees. Conor leaned back against him and tried not to purr when Alex petted his hair. Alex's touch was an addiction and he was already firmly hooked.

While they waited for their food to arrive Conor sipped his drink and listened in to the conversation as Alex chatted to the barman. "So where are the current hotspots for clubbing? I'm looking for somewhere you can have a drink, dance a bit, show off my boy."

The barman didn't have customers waiting and seemed happy to chat. *I'll bet he's happy! He wants to get his claws in my man!* Conor pushed away the little spike of jealousy. They were working and Alex was just doing his job, even if he was doing it a bit too well.

"Is The Black Orchid still the place to go? People aren't concerned about the murders?" Alex looked uninterested.

The barman shrugged. "Adds a little something to the atmosphere, I suppose, and there aren't that many decent places to go if you're into the scene. Spikes is a bit too hardcore for most and people want somewhere to move on to after they're done here. The Black Orchid is handy. Your sub here is a bit of a temptation, though, I'm surprised you let him out without a collar."

Alex stroked Conor's throat. "If we weren't working, he'd have a nice piece of leather buckled around his neck, believe me."

Conor wriggled back against Alex's body and worried at his lip. "Sir...?" he whispered.

"Yes, sweetheart? What is it?" Alex twisted him around so that they faced each other.

"Do you think Rasputin is watching people at the clubs? Picking out his victims?" Conor shivered.

"Hey now, I don't want you worrying about that, I'm here to look after you, remember? Maybe we'll go to The Black Orchid at the weekend and you'll believe you're safe with me, okay?"

"Yes, sir." Conor ducked his head. "Sorry, I didn't mean to imply..."

"No, I'm sure you didn't."

Alex's kiss took Conor by surprise. It was fierce and possessive and melted his insides into goo. The barman chuckled as he moved away to serve someone else. "Someone's going to get his arse whipped tonight!"

Conor hoped he was right.

Their food arrived and they found a small table in the corner of the crowded pub where they could eat. Neither of them spoke but Conor knew that Alex would be listening to the conversations going on around them, just as he was. Alex kept one hand on Conor's knee the whole time, making it clear that they were together without being too blatant. They finished up their sandwiches and Conor returned their empty plates and glasses to the bar where the barman gave him a wink and a "Lucky lad!"

He smiled back and nodded.

Conor didn't say very much on the walk back to the station. He leaned toward Alex and made no move to indicate that he didn't like Alex's touch on his lower back. He was aware that Alex kept looking at him and thought that Alex's normal air of confidence was just a little off. As they approached the final turn Alex took a deliberate step away from him and the short distance between their bodies felt like a gulf. Conor squared his shoulders and walked a little taller—it was becoming harder to switch from his submissive character back to his real self. *Christ! I actually enjoy submitting to him, what the hell is the matter with me?* He cast a surreptitious glance at Alex who gave him a knowing smirk in return.

"Don't worry, you can get back in character this evening," Alex teased in a low voice as they entered the station and waved to the duty sergeant. "We're not going out tonight, are we?" Conor wondered if he'd missed the memo about an operational outing. "No, we're not." Alex didn't expand but he had an expression on his face that made Conor feel like he was being stripped naked in the middle of the corridor.

"Then why...?"

"Because you like it." Alex spoke with absolute certainty. "And so do I."

He disappeared up the stairs toward his office before Conor could dispute the assertion. It would have been a lie anyway. Better to say nothing and let Alex see how far he could push — that would be much more fun.

Chapter Eight

Alex sat at the kitchen counter—paperwork spread out in front of him—and tried to concentrate. Bringing anything home from the station had been a mistake, but with the weight of work that accompanied the Rasputin case, Alex had no time for the more mundane administrative tasks that came with his rank. He had two box files worth of memos, holiday requests, statistical reports and junk mail to catch up with, but he wasn't getting very far. Conor pottered quietly around the kitchen, cleaning up after their evening meal. It wasn't the clink of china and cutlery that disturbed Alex, it was Conor's bare torso. He wore a pair of faded jeans that sat precariously on his hips and looked like they might slip at any moment. Nothing else.

"It's your own fault." Conor stretched to put some glasses away on a high shelf and Alex dropped his pen for the third time.

"What is?" Alex pretended that he didn't know what Conor was talking about.

Conor turned, rested against the cupboards and gave him a shy smile. "It wasn't my choice to be wandering around half dressed."

Alex grunted and pretended to read. "You didn't have to obey me." He looked up cautiously.

"Oh, really? Now let me recall your exact words... Hmm... Oh yes, I think you said something like 'the shirt stays off unless you want it torn into little pieces'. Or did I mishear you?"

Alex adjusted his position on his stool to accommodate his rapidly swelling cock. "I'm just practicing my character."

Conor chuckled. "You don't fool me for a minute, Alex. You don't have to role play to be dominant, it's your natural state."

Alex steepled his fingers and tried to judge whether Conor was teasing him. Conor looked calm enough. His smile was a little quirky and he was peeking from beneath his lashes in the adorable way he did when he was nervous. Alex resisted the urge to grab him and bend him over the nearest available flat surface.

"And what if that's true?" He tried to keep his voice low and unthreatening.

Conor chewed on his lower lip and stuck his hands in his pockets. "Why don't you try me and see?"

"Oh God..." Alex muttered the words before he could stop himself. Buying some time, he gathered his papers into a neat pile and put the lid on his fountain pen. There were so many things he wanted to do to the beautiful man in his kitchen, so many demands he wanted to make. The idea of Conor bending to his will, submitting to him, was a turn-on that he doubted could ever be beaten. But he needed to take it slowly. Conor might well be a natural submissive, but he was not experienced in the scene. Alex thought it unlikely that Conor had ever seen the inside of a BDSM club or playroom, but what a pleasure it would be to show him, to teach him.

"Come here and stand in front of me."

Conor moved gracefully and stood where he was told, legs slightly apart, hands clasped behind his back. For a few moments Alex indulged in just looking at him, admiring the toned musculature of Conor's chest and arms. Conor's skin was paler than his own, making his nipples stand out darkly in contrast. Alex leaned forward and flicked one little nub repeatedly until it pebbled into hardness, then gave its twin the same treatment.

"These need clamps," he mused. He trailed a finger down Conor's chest until he reached the waistband of his jeans and undid the first stud. "Take them off," he ordered, a little more sharply than intended.

Conor stared at him but didn't hesitate. He wriggled his hips until the denim slid down his legs and pooled around his ankles. He stepped out of the fabric pile and picked up the discarded garment, folding the jeans neatly and placing them on a nearby stool. Conor resumed his original position and Alex smiled. Conor's plain black underwear hugged his overexcited cock tightly and that gave Alex all the encouragement he needed to continue.

"We'll have to go shopping for some more interesting underwear for you. Plain black is fine but I'd prefer to see you in leather or latex."

Conor whimpered and shifted his weight. Alex slipped off his stool and invaded Conor's personal space. He stood as close as he could without actually touching, then very deliberately brushed the backs of his knuckles across the bulge in Conor's underwear. He leaned in and whispered in Conor's ear, "I may not allow you to come tonight. I want to see how much control you have. Obedience won't be so easy when I fill your arse and fuck you into oblivion, will it?"

Conor's strangled groan gave Alex perverse pleasure. He cupped Conor's package and squeezed lightly. "This is mine now, you don't get to touch without my permission." He pulled the waistband of Conor's shorts down and hooked it beneath his balls so that they, and Conor's rigid dick, were lewdly displayed. Conor's cheeks flushed with color. He wasn't unaffected by the way he was being treated but the fact that he remained rock hard was the vindication Alex needed. "Will that be a problem?"

"No, sir. No problem." Conor's voice was so soft, but his words were sure and steady.

Alex smiled. "Then I think we should take this to the bedroom, don't you? Keep your hands behind your back and walk in front of me."

"Like this?" Conor glanced down.

"Like that. Don't question me again."

Alex kept close behind Conor as he made his way upstairs. It gave him a perfect view of Conor's delectable arse, even though it was still covered, but also allowed him to keep his lover safe in case he stumbled. It wasn't natural for Conor to walk upstairs with his hands behind his back and much as he enjoyed controlling him, Alex also felt a burning need to protect Conor and keep him safe.

They reached the bedroom. Conor stood at the end of the bed and turned around to face Alex. He pushed his shoulders back and stood straight, meeting Alex's gaze with just a hint of challenge.

Fuck that's hot! Alex licked his lips. He couldn't wait to touch and taste but was very aware of how untried Conor was. He needed to be patient and gentle, neither of which came that easily to him. He stepped forward and pulled Conor's shorts down slowly. Conor's cock bounced as he obligingly stepped out of his underwear. Alex noted the gleam of pre-cum with satisfaction. He wrapped his fingers around Conor's length and rubbed his thumb over the leaking tip, eliciting a gasp. Conor took a step back until his thighs hit the edge of the mattress and he could retreat no farther. Alex went with him, not letting go of his prize.

"Alex, please! I'm close! If you keep holding me like that I'm going to come!"

"No. You're not." Alex squeezed the base of Conor's cock. "But perhaps I'm being unfair. You're not trained after all."

Reluctantly he released Conor's dick and crossed the room, where he pulled open the deep bottom drawer of a large wooden chest. "There should be something in here that will help you out."

"What do you mean, trained?" Conor sounded indignant. "I'm not a puppy that needs socializing!"

"I don't believe I was being particularly ambiguous, Conor. You're a submissive, and a beautiful one, but submissives need training. It'll be my pleasure to educate you." Alex found what he was looking for—a pretty red leather cock ring that would give Conor a better chance at controlling himself. Alex strolled back across the room and spoke conversationally as he fastened the strip of leather around the base of Conor's cock and balls. "This should make things easier. I wouldn't normally be this generous but control takes time to develop. Eventually, you will come only when and if I command it."

Conor looked a bit shell-shocked. "I don't... You can't... This isn't what I want." Conor made no attempt to remove the ring or step away.

"Really? You don't sound very sure of that?" Alex checked the fit of the ring and cupped Conor's balls in his palm. "I think this is *exactly* what you want."

"No..." Conor squeezed his eyes shut and Alex watched the tension and denial deepen his frown lines.

"Argue with yourself all you like, sweetheart. You need this and you're going to let me do whatever the hell I like with you." Alex fondled the heavy sac in his hand a little before stepping away to give Conor a bit of space. He paused, giving Conor every opportunity to call a halt to the scene. He grabbed a bottle of lube from a shelf and waited for Conor to open his eyes. Dark lashes fluttered and a glint of green appeared. Alex held out the lube. "Turn around, bend over the bed and prepare yourself for me."

Alex watched Conor carefully — looking for any sign at all that Conor was uncomfortable. He was definitely turned on, his rigid cock attested to that, and he was embarrassed, if the pink flush on his cheeks was anything to go by. But there was no indication that he felt he was being forced into something he didn't want. Alex was wary. This wasn't some willing twink that he'd picked up in a club where a short conversation about boundaries ensured that they both had a good time. Conor was not someone that Alex would risk hurting. Conor reached out with a trembling hand and took the lube. It took him several attempts to release the cap and when it finally snapped open he dropped it. Alex picked it up and handed it back. "Take your time. I want to watch, so give me a show."

Conor's scowl made Alex grin. His man was feeling resistant, conflicted even. Part of Conor wanted to obey but another part was clearly tempted to tell Alex to go fuck himself. He didn't speak, though, just squeezed some slippery gel onto his fingers and handed the lube back to Alex. Conor maintained eye contact with him as he rubbed his fingers together until they were slick, then finally he turned round. He bent over the bed and balanced himself with one hand. He spread his legs wide and reached back with the other hand, separating his arse cheeks with a finger and thumb.

Alex took a sharp breath as Conor spread lube around his entrance and dipped the tip of a finger inside. The lube shone, acting like a beacon for Alex's gaze. A bomb could have exploded behind him and he wouldn't have cared. He watched Conor's muscles tense then relax slowly as Conor pushed his finger deeper with an adorable whimper. Alex unzipped his trousers, gave thanks that he'd had the foresight to go without underwear, and pulled his aching cock free. He fisted himself slowly as Conor used a second finger to stretch his hole carefully.

"Oh God, Alex, please don't make me do this anymore! I need you."

"I could come just watching you touch yourself. You look so perfect, arse in the air, exposed and wanting." Alex grabbed a condom, rolled it on and coated it with lube. "I'd like to tie you down and fuck you until you scream, but you're not quite ready for that yet."

Conor withdrew his fingers and planted his other hand on the bed. He was shaking and unsteady, his breath coming in short pants.

Alex grinned. "Oh, you like that idea, don't you? You want to be restrained so that you can't escape me. You love the thought of being bound and helpless, totally at my mercy."

"No! I don't! You wouldn't?"

"I would. Definitely. And soon." Alex stripped off

his clothes and discarded them carelessly. "But that's something for you to look forward to. Now, you can tell me what you want me to do to you." Alex covered Conor's body with his own, letting him know just how hard he was. "Tell me. Beg me to fuck you."

Alex dragged his gloved cock down Conor's crack, brushing his entrance. He used his weight to pin Conor down. He might not be in bondage but Conor would know that he was being held in place with no hope of escape. "You need this. You want it so badly. Tell me how much you want me." Alex kept his voice low but forceful.

Conor gave a strangled sob. "Yes! Please, Alex, I want you to take me. Fuck me!"

Alex obliged, sliding his shaft into Conor's passage in one smooth motion. He didn't ram in but he wasn't slow either. Conor would definitely be feeling him. It might hurt a little but Alex couldn't move any slower. The tight heat of Conor's body was too enticing to resist. He stilled and stood upright, buried balls deep, and took hold of Conor's hips. "Okay?" Alex gave himself a few Brownie points for even having the willpower to keep still and ask when all he wanted to do was pound Conor's arse.

Conor fisted the bed cover and cursed, "Move, damn you! I'm not some delicate little flower..."

Alex chuckled. "Feisty little sub, aren't you? Well, you asked for it!" He held Conor hard enough to leave bruises and felt pleased at that thought. His marks needed to be on Conor's pristine skin. He jerked his hips and pressed home his claim with some force, then again and again. Beneath him, Conor made the kind of noises that just encouraged him to go harder and faster. He jerked his hips then pulled back, almost withdrawing completely before thrusting forwards again. Alex could feel the inevitable build of his orgasm as Conor's inner muscles clenched around his shaft. He was barely aware of Conor's pleas, but focused enough to hear him begging for release. "The ring, Alex, please! Take it off! I have to come!"

113

Conor was asking for permission, denying the demands of his body, and that thought drove Alex over the edge. He came in short, hot spurts, holding Conor as tightly as he dared. He pulled him closer, lifting Conor's hips from the bed and released the leather ring. Conor deserved a reward for his efforts. "Come for me, baby. Come now!"

Conor jerked in his grip and his back arched into a graceful curve as he shot over the covers, screaming Alex's name. Alex waited for the shudders to stop before he allowed himself to slip from the warm embrace of Conor's body. He left his lover draped over the bed while he disposed of the condom and fetched wet flannels to clean them both up with. Conor crawled up onto the bed and flopped, face down. Alex admired the curve of Conor's arse and stretched out next to him wrapping a proprietary arm around his waist.

"Holy fucking Christ, Alex, you've killed me," Conor muttered into his pillow. "And I'm going to feel you for a week."

Alex felt a pang of guilt and wondered if he had been too rough. Conor rolled onto his side and gazed at him. "And no you didn't hurt me. Well... You did, but in a good way. That was amazing." Conor blinked and looked away shyly. "I love it, you know, when you go all caveman on me."

"You do?"

Conor nodded and chewed on his swollen lower lip. "I'd tell you, Alex, if there was anything I didn't want."

Alex pulled Conor into his arms. He'd never been one for cuddling but with Conor everything felt different. Alex felt different. He relished the closeness and the warmth of Conor's skin pressed against him. He stroked Conor's hair and kissed the top of his head.

Conor sighed and shifted in Alex's arms. "Did you mean what you said? About wanting to tie me up?"

For a split second Alex contemplated making an excuse about the heat of the moment but Conor deserved to know. If the idea of bondage terrified him then Alex would never mention it again. "Yes, I meant it. How does that make you feel?"

Conor nuzzled closer. "I'm not sure—a little scared, nervous... But mostly turned on."

"Could you be any more perfect?" He couldn't believe how lucky he was to have found Conor and scooped him out of that filthy basement. He owed Higgs big time. "I want to tie you up, plug you... Maybe put you in chastity. I want to put your pretty nipples in clamps and spank your arse until you beg to come. I want it all... But not unless you want it too." He cuddled Conor close. "Do you understand, Conor? None of that interests me without your consent. If you want it too then I'll make you fly."

Conor chuckled. "Well, maybe not all at once, but nothing you've said makes me want to jump out of the window and run for the hills. Just..."

"Just what? You can tell me anything, Conor." Even to his own ears, Alex's voice sounded huskier than usual.

"It's just that I don't want you to think that because I like to submit to you in the bedroom I won't challenge or question you outside of it."

Alex tugged Conor's hair gently, carding it with his fingers. "Of course not. If you're not bratty outside the bedroom, what excuses will I have to punish you?"

Conor slipped his hand down and grasped Alex's cock firmly. "It'll be my pleasure to give you all the excuses you need."

Chapter Nine

Conor sat at his desk and shuffled paperwork into piles with some semblance of order. He'd done everything he could with the hospital files. He'd even gone back and retrieved some more archived materials that had been discovered in a storage locker. Every file had been examined, logged and cross-checked. Now he was left with just three possible suspects and it seemed like so little after all the work he and the team had put in. Conor pinned three dusty, slightly curled photographs to the incident board next to blown-up copies that he'd made and wrote a few bullet points beneath each of them. The three pictures were bad in a way that only passport-sized photos could be. Each of the three men looked vaguely startled, staring bug-eyed at the camera. God only knew if any of them still resembled the images on file. None of them worked at the hospital anymore and their addresses had proved useless. Conor clung to the hope that one of them was a killer and that he would be drawn out before it was too late for some other poor soul.

Even though Alex had suggested that they might pay a return visit to The Black Orchid, the trip had not materialized. There was too much work to do and no time to plan a complicated operation. After four killings there was a sense within the team that their time was running out before Rasputin struck again. The sense of dread that they might be too slow with the investigation and give Rasputin the opportunity to kill again was insidious, coloring everything they did. The weeks passed in a blur as the investigation gathered pace and all the new possibilities that Conor's link had uncovered were being explored.

Alex took Conor out to lunch as often as they could manage — frequenting all the spots that Rasputin's victims had been known to visit. They also ran in the park most mornings, carefully watched by undercover colleagues. Alex wanted where they went and what they did to be subtle but public. If they had caught Rasputin's interest then they needed to throw him a few clues. Surely a gay couple that were also investigating the case would be irresistible? They'd not publicly proclaimed that they were policemen but Conor knew damn well that the word would be out. They'd never denied it either and had no intention of keeping it a secret. Rasputin was clever and Conor knew that Alex was counting on his arrogance. That he wouldn't be able to resist the challenge.

Conor turned from the board and focused his attention on Alex who was at the front of the room delivering the regular Friday evening briefing. Conor didn't really have to listen. He already knew what Alex was going to say. They had discussed it over and over, long into the night, Alex trying desperately to come up with an alternate plan while Conor tried to convince him that there wasn't one.

"Tomorrow you all get a well-deserved day off. We have a back-up team covering the phones and picking up email here." Alex bowed slightly as he received a smattering of applause and some desultory whistles. "However..." That brought a chorus of groans in response. "Tomorrow night we go back to The Black Orchid. You've heard the plan and you know what to do. You all need to be in place by nine p.m. It's crunch time — we can't sit on our arses any longer waiting for this psycho to strike. It's time to take the game to him." He paused and glanced around the room, meeting the eyes of every man present. When it was his turn, Conor felt like Alex's gaze was burning holes right through him. He nodded slightly, trying to convey that he understood Alex's conflict but agreed that they had to do something provocative. Alex looked away and asked, "Any questions, anyone?"

There was some shuffling and fidgeting, but no questions. They'd been over the plan time and time again until every man and woman involved could recite it backwards. Alex and Conor would spend the evening at the club. They would fake a lovers' quarrel and Conor would leave the club alone. They were hoping that the temptation would prove too great for Rasputin to ignore and that he would attempt to take Conor. Then the jaws of the trap would close. They had gone over every scenario, mitigated every possible risk, but Conor still had a sick feeling in the pit of his stomach. Even if he was right about one of the three suspects he'd identified, the team had been unable to track them down. The three men were ghosts. He just could not see any other way to take control of the game and he had been instrumental in convincing Alex to go ahead. Their relationship, and any worries Alex had about Conor's safety, had to be put aside so that they could do their jobs.

The team gradually disbanded, heading off to spend some much needed time with friends and family. Conor watched Alex have a few words with each of them, taking time to insure that everyone was comfortable and that they knew how important their roles were, however small. Conor smiled. Alex was a great boss and an excellent detective. He was an even better lover. Conor cast secret glances Alex's way — he loved to just look at him. Alex radiated strength. He could make Conor feel safe just by being in the same room. But what Conor loved the most was the way Alex's icy blue eyes warmed only for him.

Conor scraped his chair back and stood to stare again at the three suspect photos pinned to the incident board. Three possibilities. He ran over the scant facts in his head.

Saul Fletcher, thirty-five, two arrests for assaults on gay men, five years in prison for attempted rape. Known to associate with white extremist groups. Had been dismissed from his hospital warehouse role for non-disclosure of his conviction. No known permanent address.

Cyril Bates, forty-three, single. Short, overweight and the product of an abusive single mother, Bates had spent much of his childhood in and out of foster care and group homes. He'd worked as a lab technician at the hospital until a male nurse had accused him of sexual harassment. There must have been some foundation to the charge because Bates had resigned before he could be pushed. No longer resident at last known address.

Donovan Leary, known as Van, aged twenty-nine. A wannabe drug pusher who'd been caught stealing from hospital stores. Notes on his record called him sly and manipulative. Two arrests prior to the incident at the hospital, but no convictions. He'd gotten away with a caution for the thefts. He'd been caught on security cameras at The Black Orchid and was suspected of beating up a couple of young lads that he'd picked up there. Current address vacated recently.

Their faces were seared into Conor's brain. If any of them put in an appearance at The Black Orchid on Saturday night they would be followed, but what if he was wrong? None of the suspects were men he'd want to meet down a dark alley, but nothing on their records indicated a propensity for serial murder. What he knew had been gleaned from sketchy personnel files, social services and criminal databases. He could make assumptions but Conor knew all too well how dangerous that was. When it came down to it, all he had were gut feelings and very few hard facts.

"What if I've missed something?" Conor whispered to himself.

"We've done everything we can. Stop worrying. This is a team effort, even though I know you feel responsible," Alex said. He crossed the room and squeezed Conor's shoulder gently. "It's time for us to go home too. We deserve a break as much as the rest of them."

Conor nodded, leaning into Alex's solid body. "Okay."

"Good. I'm taking you out tonight, so I hope you saved a little bit of energy."

"Are you asking me out on a date, sir?" Conor teased.

From the glare he received, Conor felt a bit like a mouse that had been cornered by a particularly sadistic cat.

"I'm not asking you, I'm telling you," Alex responded.

Conor smiled. Maybe the moggy wasn't sadistic, just cantankerous and a little embarrassed to be courting his prey.

"Well, in that case, how can I refuse?"

"You can't," Alex grouched.

Conor smiled serenely. "You are so hot when you're grumpy."

They packed up quickly and Alex drove across town. He parked and Conor followed him down a narrow cobbled lane. They were in the old part of the town where the buildings seemed to lean precariously toward one another. Some of them were half-timbered and dated from the 1600s. In the daylight, tourists wandered, exclaiming the area to be 'quaint', but by night it was just a little creepy. Conor laughed at himself — the brave policeman spooked by a few shadows and the amber glint of an urban fox's eyes.

The tiny restaurant was virtually invisible. He narrowly avoided colliding with Alex as he came to a dead stop in front of a polished wooden door with a small lamp above it. There was no menu outside on the wall, just a small brass plate that read 'Dionysus'.

"Here we are. This is my favorite place to eat. The food's amazing." Alex turned back to look at Conor.

"I didn't realize you were a foodie." Conor enjoyed Alex's obvious enthusiasm.

"Oh I'm not. Not really. But the food really is good here and the owners are not going to object to me holding your hand across the table."

Conor felt warm inside at the thought that Alex wanted to hold his hand. There was definitely a soppy romantic under that macho exterior.

Inside, subtle lighting and lattice screens entwined with greenery gave each of the six tables complete privacy. A waiter took them to the only unoccupied table and handed them leather-bound menus as they sat down.

"Good evening, Mr Courtney, it's a pleasure to see you. It's been a while."

"Good evening, Will, it's good to be here." Alex smiled at the waiter warmly. "If you could bring us some mineral water?"

"Of course, sir." Will moved away silently.

"You come here often enough to be on first name terms with the waiter?" Conor felt just a little jealous.

"Will's engaged to one of Higgs' nieces. He's practically family. You don't need to worry." Alex seemed amused.

"I'm not worried... Just... Oh never mind." Conor examined the menu very closely. When he peeked up, Alex was looking right at him. Candlelight flickered and tiny points of gold danced in Alex's pale eyes. Conor was entranced by the play of flickering shadows across Alex's face. Feeling suddenly shy, Conor dipped his lashes, cast his eyes down again and felt the flush rise on his cheeks.

"Stop staring at me!"

Alex chuckled, the sound rich and warm. "Why? You're the prettiest thing in here, and I like to look at you."

Alex pulled Conor's hand onto the table and started to play with his fingers, stroking them before finally entwining their hands together. "We've had so little time alone. I feel like I know you well, but actually you've never told me anything about yourself. Do you have any family?"

Conor looked up. "Not anymore. My parents died in a car wreck when I was three, I don't remember them at all. I was brought up by my maternal grandparents, and believe me this isn't a sob story—I had the best childhood. But my mother was a late baby and my grandparents were quite elderly—they both passed away in the last couple of years. My father's parents were already gone and it was a small family. It's just me now. How about you?"

Alex gave an undignified snort. "Three older brothers. All married with growing broods of assorted children that my parents spoil rotten at any and every opportunity. I see them at Christmas, sometimes in the summer — but I moved here for work and it's a bit of a haul to visit because they all live in the north, mostly Northumberland."

"Do your parents know that you're gay?"

"Since I was sixteen. Fortunately my brothers have more than fulfilled the grandchild quota. My dad was a bit shocked at first but he just wants to see me happy. My mum and sisters-in-law seem to think that it's their sworn duty to find me a decent man. My brothers couldn't care less. When we were in our late teens it just meant less competition for the ladies. Once the girls at school knew I batted for the other team, I suddenly became popular. I got some grief from a few of the boys but I was big enough to take care of myself. My brothers took full advantage — going out with me was almost as effective as pushing a baby in a pram or walking a cute puppy."

Conor choked back a laugh as Alex continued, "Now they are more interested in taking the piss out of me because I'm on the force. I could write a book with the number of police-related jokes they churn out every time I see them."

"They sound great." Conor felt a little regretful. "My grandparents never knew about me — there never seemed to be a right time to tell them. It's not as if I was always bringing boyfriends home or anything."

"You must have had plenty of offers…" Alex's question was unspoken but Conor answered it anyway. "I've never been interested in a superficial fuck. A lot of men can't see past the way I look." He said it in a way that was coldly factual and nothing to do with vanity.

"How do you know I'm not one of them?" Alex asked. "It's no secret that I think you are absolutely stunning."

Conor swallowed and tried to tug his fingers out of Alex's grasp, to no avail. "Alex! You shouldn't say things like that!"

Alex just held his hand tighter. "Why not. I'm not going to hide the truth, so how do you know?"

"I trust you. You care too much — about everything. You are the most intense person I've ever met, Alex. I feel like you know what I'm thinking, what I need."

It was Alex's turn to blush. Conor grinned at the reaction because it just confirmed everything he'd just said.

"I hope I live up to your expectations," Alex said seriously.

"We've got plenty of time to find out." Conor flapped a menu with his free hand. "Now can we order? I'm starving!"

The service was attentive but not intrusive, the food elegantly simple. After a brief discussion about Conor's likes and dislikes, Alex ordered for both of them and Conor didn't object. They ate scallops laced with truffle oil, then shared a baked fish dish and an amazing salad that even had flower petals in it. Gentle music played in the background and hushed conversations continued around them, but Conor was totally absorbed in Alex. They talked and laughed and held hands and, for a while, the real world went away and left them in peace.

"Would you like dessert?" Alex asked, far too innocently. Conor debated in his head whether to request dessert, then cheese, then coffee and mints. Though it would be fun to torment Alex and make him wait, Conor wanted to get home just as urgently as he suspected Alex did.

"Definitely," Conor replied. "Something nice and creamy. But I don't think what I want is on the menu here."

"Nice and... Jesus!" Alex paid the bill with indecent haste and headed for the door. Conor wasn't far behind. It had started to rain. In fact the heavens had opened and there was a torrential downpour going on. By the time they had sprinted the short distance to the car they were both soaked to the skin. Conor's long hair sent uncomfortable drips down inside his collar. Droplets soaked his shirt making it cling horribly to his skin.

* * * *

The car's powerful heater meant that by the time Alex had

driven them home and parked up, Conor was more damp than wet and his shivers had little to do with the cold. He peeled himself away from the leather seat and clambered out of the car. The rain had eased but it was still enough for him to run for the front door and breathe a huge sigh of relief when Alex pushed it open and they both staggered into the warmth of the hall.

They dumped soggy shoes and socks in the hall cupboard. Alex ducked into the cloakroom to grab a towel and they both gave their hair a cursory rub. Alex piled kindling and logs into the fireplace in the lounge and coaxed tiny licks of flame into a roaring blaze. As soon as the fire was established, he stacked it with logs and sat on the floor, back against an armchair, and sank his bare feet into the hearth rug. Alex parted his legs and patted the rug.

The first little frisson of defiance he felt as he was told where to sit fizzled out instantly. Conor positioned himself in between Alex's legs and shuffled backwards until he could lean against Alex's chest.

"Ugh! That's cold!" With both of them wearing clammy shirts, the contact made Conor squirm. "Then I'd better do something about it." Alex wrapped his arms around Conor's waist from behind and proceeded to slowly unbutton Conor's shirt. Conor lifted the damp mass of his hair out of the way and Alex planted soft kisses on his exposed neck. Conor had to resist the urge to purr like a contented cat. Between the warmth of the fire and Alex's lips on his skin, he was in heaven.

Alex smelled of rain and the light citrus scent of his favorite body wash. Conor's senses neared overload as Alex ran his tongue along the ridge of Conor's collarbone, then bit down gently on the juncture of his neck and shoulder. Alex sucked hard and Conor knew he was being marked. Just the thought that Alex was claiming ownership made Conor's cock harden to aching point. Conor's entire body shivered with desire and Alex's low, husky chuckle revealed his pleasure at the effect he was having.

Conor held his breath as Alex ran his hands across his chest, teasing erect nipples with the softest caress. Alex pushed him gently forwards, then peeled damp fabric backwards until he could pull the shirt off. It felt good to be rid of the clinging material. His skin was cool but gradually warming in the heat of the fire and his hair was drying quickly. The flames crackled as Alex massaged Conor's neck and shoulders with deft strokes until Conor relaxed completely under his ministrations. Alex had strong hands — his fingers pressed hard and deep into tense muscle, finding knots that Conor hadn't even realized were there. By the time Alex had finished working on him, Conor was drowsing happily. Alex wrapped strong arms around him and for a while they just sat, enjoying the closeness and the quiet.

Conor loved the feeling of being imprisoned by Alex's arms, so safe, so secure, but he craved the sensation of skin against skin and Alex was still wearing his shirt. He pushed gently against Alex's arms until he was released then turned and knelt in front of him, leaning forward to unbutton Alex's top. Alex shrugged it off and threw it onto the chair behind him. Conor drank in the view of golden skin, shimmering in the firelight. He couldn't resist a taste and leaned forward to lap at Alex's nipples, hardening each in turn before kissing the gentle valley between Alex's pectoral muscles.

"You taste good, better than dessert," he murmured before turning around and relaxing back against Alex's body again. Alex embraced him and nuzzled the curve of his neck. Conor took hold of the arm around his waist and pulled Alex's hand up so that he could gently suckle each fingertip in turn. He kissed Alex's palm softly, then brushed his tongue across the sensitive skin on Alex's inner wrist. Alex's muscles flexed involuntarily, pinning Conor tighter. Alex's cock nudged against his lower back, rock hard and twitching. He smiled, happy that Alex was turned on too. Conor's cock danced to its own personal tune, fighting the confines of his underwear. As if sensing his need Alex reached down and slipped open the button on Conor's waistband. As he lowered the zip beneath it, Alex's hand brushed against Conor's bulge too firmly for the contact to have been accidental. Conor jerked and moaned softly. He lifted his arse off the floor then with one swift motion removed his trousers and threw them aside.

Alex gave an annoyed grunt and slid one finger under the waistband of Conor's shorts, torturing the skin beneath with little strokes.

"Get rid of them or I'll rip them off."

Alex's tone was mild but Conor had absolutely no doubt that he meant it. He lifted his arse off the floor again, allowing Alex to roll the offending garment down to his thighs. Conor's cock sprang up, gleaming with the moisture of his arousal, bobbing excitedly as he shoved his underwear farther down his legs until he could kick them away.

Still pinned in place by Alex's arm, Conor couldn't escape as Alex slid his free hand down between his parted legs. He stroked the inside of Conor's upper thighs one at a time, then palmed his balls.

"Mmm. So hot." Alex squeezed gently and rubbed with his thumb at the same time.

"Oh Christ!" Conor fought Alex's hold but couldn't get away. "I'm going to come, Alex, stop!"

Alex snickered. "Now why would I want to do that? You're my prisoner and I get to do whatever I like with you."

Conor struggled against Alex's restraining arm but there was no way Alex was going to let him loose until he'd completed his mission.

"Fight me all you want, sweetheart, it won't do you any good but I kind of enjoy it," Alex growled. He gripped Conor's jerking cock, rolled his thumb over the head and pushed his nail into the little slit.

"Did you know that you can get rings that sit here?" Alex

126

circled the point where the head of Conor's cock narrowed. "And have a little ball that sits just here?" Alex pressed Conor's slit again. "Or there are rods called sounds that slip right inside."

Conor gulped and wondered why the idea of Alex sliding a foreign object inside his cock was making him even harder. Then it got difficult to think at all because Alex was jacking him hard. Friction added to the heat already present and Conor slammed his head back against Alex's chest, breathing in short, rapid gasps. There was no going back now. Alex moved his hand faster. Conor felt the nip of teeth on his earlobe before Alex lapped at the soft skin beneath it. Then his nipples were pinched and rolled in turn. The combined sensations pushed Conor over the edge. His hips bucked and he shot across the rug with a cry of ecstasy.

"I need to be inside you." Alex's voice was rough with desire. "Now!"

Still panting, Conor swiveled around to face his lover, kneeling between his thighs. Alex was flushed and gorgeous, his eyes darkened with lust. Conor managed to coordinate his movements enough to lean forward and unfasten Alex's trousers. Clumsily he pulled them down, taking Alex's briefs along for the ride.

"Oh! Oh, that's just beautiful!" Conor gaped at Alex's straining erection in admiration. He dragged his gaze up to hard abs, sheened with perspiration, and realized that there was a soppy grin pasted on his face. It was better than winning the lottery, knowing that Alex was his and that he was Alex's.

"Tell me what you want, Alex," Conor whispered.

Alex narrowed his eyes. "There aren't enough hours in the day for me to describe exactly what I would like to do to you, and now's not the time for talking. Come here."

Conor knew what Alex wanted. He straddled Alex's thighs, rising up on his knees until he was stretched wide. The tip of Alex's cock was scant inches from his arse. He lowered himself until the end of Alex's cock grazed his hole.

"Wait!" Alex's voice was anguished. "I haven't stretched you. Need to prepare you first. Shit, the nearest lube's in the kitchen and we need a condom."

Conor reached for his discarded trousers and fumbled in the pocket until he found the sachet of lube he'd stashed there. He held it up triumphantly. "You get tested for work, yes? You're clean?"

Alex nodded, looking a little wide-eyed.

"Well, so am I." Conor ripped open the foil sachet with his teeth and squeezed the contents onto his fingers. He spread the cool gel over Alex's thick shaft and rubbed a little over and into his own pucker. "I trust you. I want to feel you. Is that okay with you?"

"Is that...? Fuck, Conor, of course it's okay. But wait—I don't want to hurt you." He dragged a finger through the lube on his cock and applied it quickly to Conor's hole, sliding in fast and deep. He added a second finger far too quickly, but Conor loved his impatience.

"Enough already!"

Alex removed his fingers. "Demanding brat!" He groaned as Conor descended onto his cock. Without much preparation Conor felt the burn.

"Tell me if it hurts, Conor," Alex ordered but Conor enjoyed the friction. He impaled himself until he'd taken the whole of Alex's length inside. It hurt, but the pain was nothing to the pleasure that came with it. His inner muscles clenched tighter as he leaned forward and wrapped his arms around Alex's neck, settling onto his lap.

"Fuck, it's like a vice in there, are you sure you're all right?" Alex sounded hoarse.

"I'm fine. Better than fine! Perfect." Conor wiggled his hips and kissed Alex hard, then he let go and settled backwards, arching his spine until his groin was thrust forward and his weight was resting on his hands. The angle meant that Alex's cock pressed hard on Conor's prostate. Sparks of heat shot through him and his cock hardened again. Alex shifted and Conor moaned at the sensation. Eyes welling with emotional tears, he lifted himself up and dropped back, slamming into Alex's lap.

Alex swore creatively and Conor took that as tacit agreement to continue. His thighs ached as he moved himself up and down. The angle of Alex's cock inside him touched pleasure points that he hadn't known existed. When Conor thought he couldn't carry on, Alex took over, grasping Conor's hips and lifting him up so that Alex could buck upwards and spear him even deeper. Alex slid down from his resting place against the chair so that he was flat on the floor, knees raised. Conor rode him hard, teeth clenched and eyes closed, fully hard again.

"Fill me, Alex, come inside me," Conor gasped the words.

Alex obliged with a yell and the warmth of Alex's release flooded his channel. Almost simultaneously, Conor came as well, coating Alex's chest with cum. Still joined, Conor collapsed on top of Alex, shaking uncontrollably.

Neither of them spoke. Eventually Conor detached himself and lay on his front next to Alex, head propped in his hands. The fire crackled and popped, sparks flying.

"That was just...amazing! Have you ever bare-backed before?"

Alex looked a bit dazed. "No. First time. You've ruined me for anything else from now on."

Conor chuckled. "Good." He shifted farther away from the intense heat of the fire. "I'm going to take a shower before my arse catches fire in a whole new way," he grumbled.

Alex mumbled something incoherent. He reached over and stroked Conor's backside, then without warning sank a finger inside his channel and wiggled it around. Conor gasped and squirmed. "What are you doing?"

"Checking your heat levels." Alex withdrew his finger and squeezed Conor's balls hard enough to make Conor squeak.

"What was that for?" Conor protested half-heartedly, enjoying the combination of pleasure and pain that Alex was treating him to.

"Topping from the bottom, bossy brat." Alex grinned smugly. "If I had more energy I'd take you over my knee and give you a spanking, but I think you've broken me."

Conor scooted away as quickly as he could and clambered to his feet. "Need to shower…" he stuttered as he made his escape. The last thing he heard as he headed for the stairs was Alex's chuckle and a sultry, "You'll keep, gorgeous."

Chapter Ten

Conor awoke with a start, wondering vaguely what had pushed him so abruptly from his dreams. He was irritated because he'd been having a particularly good dream involving Alex, a set of handcuffs and some chocolate mousse. He sighed, then winced as light flashed across the room, stabbing at his newly opened eyes. The light was followed by a low, threatening rumble and Conor realized that a storm was underway. Rain lashed the bedroom window and the wind howled through the trees outside.

Conor wanted nothing more than to snuggle back under the covers, press himself against Alex's warm body and get back to his dream, but physical needs drove him to the bathroom. He rinsed his face and cleaned his teeth then headed back to bed.

Alex was awake looking deliciously tousled and sleepy. A crack of thunder rattled the window panes.

"Who's making all that fucking racket?"

Alex was definitely not a morning person. Conor grinned as Alex pulled the covers over his head and hid.

"Well, you could take it personally and assume that Thor doesn't like you. Or you could go with a more scientific explanation and accept that the cumulonimbi are giving off electrical discharges. Either way, it's a great excuse for staying in bed."

Conor slipped back under the covers and lay on his front, chin on his arms.

"Smart arse."

"Ouch!" Conor yelped as Alex slapped the aforementioned arse.

"My hand on your backside feels so good, I might just have to do that again."

Before Conor could roll out of the way, he was firmly spanked again.

"Hey! What the hell, Alex?" Conor protested weakly, his skin smarting and his cock swelling.

Alex swung himself out of bed, yanked back the covers and gave Conor three more swats. Conor's face burned as he found himself pushing back toward Alex's hand, seeking more contact. Alex chuckled and obliged with a couple more hits.

"You should see how pretty you arse looks, all pink and glowing. I can feel the heat coming off your skin."

"I'm glad you're enjoying yourself!" Conor rolled onto his side.

"And you're not? I warned you last night that you needed a spanking." Alex leaned across the bed and grabbed Conor's stiff dick. "This tells me you're loving it!"

Conor couldn't help himself. He wanted more and jerked his hips so that his cock pushed through Alex's fist.

"Oh no you don't!"

Conor pouted as Alex let go of him and backed away.

"And don't give me that hurt puppy look either."

Conor rolled onto his back, spread his legs and stroked himself. He nibbled on his lower lip and batted his eyelashes at Alex shamelessly.

Alex froze, mouth open, eyes glazing. "Jesus!" He jolted himself into motion, stalked to the bedside cabinet and pulled a pair of handcuffs from the drawer. Before Conor could do more than squeak, his wrists were cuffed to the headboard.

Alex shook his head in a reprimand, and headed for the bathroom without a word. He returned, a few minutes later, shrugging into a thick blue robe. "I need energy before I deal with you properly. What would you like for breakfast?"

Conor squirmed and tugged on the cuffs, making the

chain rattle. He was hard to the point of pain.

"How can you even think about breakfast? You can't leave me here like this!"

"Oh, believe me I can." Alex looked stern. "I'm going to keep you frustrated and wanting for as long as I choose. In the meantime, you can either tell me what you want to eat or go hungry."

Conor pouted some more. "Whatever you're having is fine."

Alex gave an evil chuckle. "Oh, I'm having you. But I have an indecent craving for a bacon sandwich first. Don't go anywhere."

"Funny."

Alex disappeared.

Conor slumped on his pillow and peered the length of his body at his swaying erection. "Oh God, I hope he cooks fast!"

Tantalizing smells began drifting up the stairs. Conor loved the smell of cooking bacon and his mouth watered. It wasn't enough to take his mind off the fact that Alex had chained him to the bed, or that he really, really liked the way it made him feel. His cock hadn't lost any of its stiffness—in fact, thinking about being helpless and at Alex's mercy just seemed to make him harder. *Think I may have discovered my kinky side*. He had a pretty good idea that Alex would take great delight in helping him explore it further. If that were the case, then Conor wouldn't object. All the things that Alex had said he wanted to do to him ran through Conor's mind. "Jesus, stop tormenting yourself!" Conor realized that he'd spoken out loud but he couldn't help it. Handcuffs were one thing, but what if the key Alex had in his dressing gown pocket was the key to a cock cage? How would that make him feel? Apparently, even harder. His dick ached and his balls were on fire. Not being able to touch was the ultimate frustration. He could shout out, Alex had left the door open, but Conor knew he wouldn't. He was stronger than that and he wanted Alex to know it.

After what seemed like an eternity but was probably little more than ten minutes, Alex returned with a tray laden with glasses of freshly squeezed orange juice and plates of bacon sandwiches.

"Oh my! Someone really likes being tied up!" His words were a verbal smirk. "You look hard as iron."

Conor scowled. "Let me go, Alex."

Alex set the tray on the bed and grinned. "Why? You look absolutely delicious. Nearly as edible as these bacon sandwiches."

"Alex!" Conor didn't appreciate being compared to breakfast. He was stretched out, naked, hard and probably blushing from head to toe.

"If I free you, you have to promise not to touch yourself. If you do, I'll chain you up again and feed you myself."

Conor was torn between belligerence and the signals his grumbling stomach was sending to his brain. "Fine. I promise."

"That was easy." Alex sounded suspicious.

"I love bacon sandwiches. They are worth a bit of a dent to my pride." Conor shrugged as Alex unlocked the cuffs and released him. "But I still can't believe you chained me up... Without so much as a by your leave."

Alex twirled the cuffs on a finger. "Somehow I don't think the effect would have been quite the same if I'd asked first, would it?"

Conor grunted but didn't confirm or deny Alex's statement. It felt dangerous to admit just how much Alex's dominance turned him on. They'd known each other just a few short weeks and deep down Conor worried that what he was feeling was a side effect of their involvement in the Rasputin investigation and the roles they had to play. He pulled the covers back up to his waist. "Not touching! Promise!" He held his hands up above the bed to show that he wasn't being naughty.

The bread was thick and white with a nice chewy crust, properly buttered with a smear of ketchup. The bacon was crispy round the edges but tender in the middle. Conor swallowed his last delicious mouthful, smacked his lips in appreciation and flipped back onto his stomach.

"Fantastic! Practically orgasmic," he proclaimed, wiggling his arse provocatively.

Alex's eyes darkened a shade or two. "I can think of better ways to turn you to jelly, though. Now, where was I?" Alex planted another firm slap across Conor's backside, which was already nicely warmed.

"Oh yes, you were being cheeky and I was going to make you beg for mercy." His voice was low and growly. Conor loved it—the sound rumbled through his body and made him shiver. He craved the sting of Alex's hand on his behind.

Alex pulled Conor's arse cheeks apart, pressed one slightly buttery finger into his hole and held it there. Conor held his breath, desperately willing Alex to move, add another one, anything. He pushed back but Alex moved with him. Conor moaned softly. Alex stroked his channel, but it wasn't enough, he needed more.

"Say you're sorry," Alex said quietly.

"Screw you." Conor's words were clear enough despite being muffled by his pillow, where he'd buried his head in frustration.

"Patience, I'm coming to that—screwing you, that is—but first you need to apologize for being a brat." Alex thrust a second finger into Conor's channel and stretched him slowly. "You don't seem particularly remorseful."

"Oh God!" Conor groaned pitifully. Alex's scissored the fingers inside him, but far too slowly.

Lightning flashed and Alex laughed like the villain in a particularly bad horror movie, "I'm afraid praying isn't going to help you. Not even to Thor."

Conor bit his pillow as Alex thrust a third digit into his hole and grabbed his balls. Alex began to squeeze the soft flesh in concert with the thunder.

Conor squealed. It wasn't a sound he was proud of, but

he was beyond caring. "Please, Alex! I'm sorry! For Christ's sake fuck me—I can't stand any more!" Conor squirmed, his rock-hard cock trapped beneath him. It was as if Alex hadn't heard a word, he just kept probing and squeezing. Conor's balls tightened and he knew he was going to come, it was inevitable with all the stimulation he was getting, but then Alex squeezed the base of his shaft and his orgasm was rudely interrupted. Something in his brain short-circuited at the denial.

"You son of a bitch! Fuck me, you bastard!" Conor yelled.

Alex withdrew his fingers and flipped Conor onto his back. Conor discovered he was more flexible than he thought as Alex pushed his bent legs back to gain better access. Alex had grabbed lube from somewhere. He applied a cursory finger-full and slid his cock into place. Conor hissed at the rapid penetration and tried to relax as Alex gripped his hips hard. Alex's restraint was amazing as he stilled but that wasn't what Conor wanted. He gave his lover the go-ahead with a strangled, "Please!" He needed rough and hard. He wanted to be taken.

Conor looked into Alex's narrowed eyes and saw the glint of desire just before Alex slammed forwards, driving himself deeper than Conor had thought possible. One of them gasped, Conor wasn't sure whom. It was taking all his will not to beg and cry for more. Alex lifted one of Conor's legs onto his shoulder and bent over him. He took his wrists and held them down with all his weight. He thrust again and Conor whimpered—the new angle ensuring that Alex hit his prostate with perfect precision.

"Like that?" Alex growled but didn't wait for a response. Not that Conor was even capable of saying anything intelligible. Alex took him roughly then, hard and without mercy, pounding his arse with desperate force. Conor pushed against the iron grip on his wrists, his head thrown back as far as the pillows would allow. A huge crack of thunder drowned his scream as he climaxed in a red fog of agony and rapture. Seconds later, with one final powerful thrust, Alex pulsed into him, screaming his name.

Alex collapsed next to Conor and it was a full five minutes before a tousled blond head lifted. Alex's eyes had regained their usual pale blue shade.

"Are you okay? I wasn't really in control, did I hurt you?"

Conor immediately reassured him with a gentle smile. He didn't want Alex to be worried about anything. Conor twisted toward him and couldn't hide his wince at the ache of bruises that were beginning to develop on the flesh of his hips where Alex had gripped him.

"I'm sorry... I went too far..." Alex sounded heartbroken.

Conor pulled Alex into a hug and whispered into his ear, "That was incredible. You are the best thing that ever happened to me. You don't need to hold back, ever. You gave me exactly what I wanted."

Tentatively Alex responded and held Conor just as tightly, "Sure?"

"Absolutely. When can we do that again?"

Alex chuckled into Conor's neck, then replaced the laugh with kisses. "Soon. Very soon."

* * * *

The storm finally stopped rumbling around midday but it remained overcast. The sky was low, dark and angry, threatening more rain that never came. Conor and Alex sprawled in front of the fire, read the papers, drank too much coffee and talked about anything and everything except what they had to do that night. They kissed and touched but went no further, it was enough just to be together.

By early evening, the phone started ringing as their colleagues began calling in with updates on all aspects of the operation. When Higgs called, Alex put the phone onto loud speaker so that they could both hear what was going on. "Hey, boss, just wanted to let you know that one of Conor's three suspects, Saul Fletcher, has been picked up for drunk driving in an untaxed car with no insurance. He's

137

safely under lock and key."

"That's great, Higgs, that only leaves two faces to keep an eye out for—Cyril Bates and Van Leary. That'll make things a little bit simpler to manage."

"Agreed. It's a good omen."

"You superstitious old git." Alex laughed.

"Hey, don't mock," Conor chimed in. "I'll take any advantage going."

"Quite right, lad, you tell him." Higgs chortled. "We've got all the local beat officers on high alert and any available detectives are checking every gay hangout in the city for anything or anyone suspicious. If anyone even twitches funny in one of those places we'll know about it."

"And everything's in place at The Black Orchid?" Alex asked. It was a big operation involving a lot of personnel from various different divisions and he had more reason than most to want to be sure that his plans were being implemented to the letter.

"Yes, boss. Just like the last time you asked me. And the time before that."

Conor coughed back a laugh.

"Funny. Go and get yourself some coffee, Higgs. I don't want you dropping off later when it's past your bedtime."

"Yes, sir. Anything you say, sir." Higgs rang off, laughing.

* * * *

At eight thirty, Conor left Alex to his worrying and went to get ready for the night. As he showered and shaved he had to admit that the queasy knot in his stomach was nothing to do with anything he'd eaten that day. He told himself that it was good to be nervous. Complacency would more than likely get him killed. He concentrated on the mundane actions required and gradually his nausea receded into calm acceptance. He had a job to do and he would do it to the best of his ability. It was just another undercover operation and he had been involved in plenty of those before.

More clothes from Alex's shopping trip were laid out for him on their bed. Alex must have put them there while Conor had been in the shower. Conor glared at the garments as if staring at them could change them into something less... Less... He didn't even know how to express what he wanted to turn them into. Their only redeeming characteristic was that they were black. Conor sighed. "I can't believe I really have to wear this stuff."

"Well, you do." Alex lounged in the doorway smirking. His clothes were also black, but far more conservative.

"Fine," Conor snapped. He dropped the towel that was slung around his hips and bent forward to pick up transparent underwear that was about as far from comfort and practicality as it was possible to get. He could feel Alex's gaze practically burning into his arse and his heart rate accelerated. He was in a very provocative position and he knew it. He wiggled his backside a little and Alex cursed.

"All right, you've had your revenge. Put something on already!" Alex's voice sounded a little clipped.

Conor grinned over his shoulder. "Serves you bloody well right!"

He pulled on the briefs, followed by tight black leather trousers that were laced down the side seams. The leather was beautifully soft and molded to his shape. The placket was fastened by criss-crossed leather thongs and didn't feel particularly secure. Alex must have read his mind because when Conor turned to face him Alex's line of sight was firmly at crotch level. "Nice and easy to access," Alex commented happily.

"Fuck off." It wasn't imaginative but the clothing made him feel vulnerable and he didn't like it.

The loose black shirt that he put on next harked back to a more romantic era, but as he turned to the light Conor realized that it was translucent. He was fully clothed but felt completely naked. He sat shakily on the edge of the bed to put on his boots then stood and dealt with his damp hair, pulling it back into a loose tail with a black ribbon. He turned to face Alex.

"Bloody hell, you look completely edible!"

Conor shifted uncomfortably, wondering if he was being teased. "You really like it?"

"I do." He pulled the same slim leather collar from his pocket that Conor had worn before and fastened it around Conor's neck.

Alex ran his tongue over his lips slowly and deliberately. "When this is over, you can wear these clothes again—just for me."

"Even this?" Conor touched his neck.

"Especially that. It suits you. And I'll take you somewhere where everyone will know that it means you belong to me." Alex took the eyeliner pencil from Conor's shaking hand and applied it deftly. "There. You look perfect."

Conor gazed at him, memorizing the planes and angles of his face, the golden glint of his hair. He wanted to imprint Alex on his mind in case anything went wrong.

Alex took a step back and smiled reassuringly. "We're ready. We've done everything we can and when this is all over, we can be together without all the drama."

"You promise?" Conor felt young and insecure, he wished he had Alex's confidence. It was ridiculous. He was an experienced undercover detective. This was not his first time working in a dangerous situation, but somehow the odds seemed stacked against them. A future with Alex was a big prize that felt completely out of reach.

"I promise." Alex said it with absolute certainty and even though Conor knew that such a promise might be impossible to keep, those two small words gave him hope.

Down in the hall they pulled on leather jackets and gauntlets and prepared to leave.

"Now, are you sure you don't mind me using the bike?" Alex asked for about the fifth time that day.

Conor grimaced. "You know I don't mind. I'm not especially looking forward to riding pillion like a girl, but I "suppose it fits the image."

"No girl could ever look as hot as you're going to, sat behind me. I just hope I can concentrate on the road with you pressed to my back." Alex grinned cheekily, "You in leather are a walking wet dream."

Conor ducked his head but Alex turned and cupped Conor's face in his hands, tilting his chin up. "Remember, what I do and say once we get to the club isn't real." His kiss was gentle and loving. Conor's breath hitched—he'd never thought of Alex in those terms before. Did Alex love him? Now was not the time to even be considering such things. Conor clamped down on his emotions and focused on the job in hand.

"When you leave the club tonight, Conor, be careful. Promise me," Alex said urgently.

Conor wasn't stupid, he had no intention of taking unnecessary risks, but even as he whispered "I promise" he knew it was another vow that might have to be broken.

Together they walked out into the rain.

Chapter Eleven

The roads were slick and greasy — little rainbows flashed in the oily patches as they sped along. Alex handled the powerful bike with confidence and skill, riding quickly but safely through empty streets. An occasional pedestrian hurried along the glistening pavements, head bent against the rain, scurrying for the warmth of home. There was very little traffic, just a few cars, wipers fighting to keep windscreens clear, drivers squinting through the spray. Conor wrapped his arms around Alex's waist and held on, pressed close. Even through his visor he could smell the leather of Alex's jacket and it calmed him. He enjoyed the contact while it lasted, letting the familiar rumble of the bike's engine settle his nerves.

The journey didn't take nearly long enough. Conor would have been happy to keep going straight out of town to wherever a tank of fuel took them, but he wasn't the one deciding on their destination. Reluctantly he relinquished his hold on Alex and swung his leg over the bike. Alex propped it in a space not far from the club's main door, under the amber glow of a streetlight. They left their helmets, jackets and gloves at the club's small cloakroom and headed inside. Two of the bouncers were actually undercover policemen, as were a couple of the bar staff. Alex had begged and borrowed colleagues from several departments — trawling for those who could pull off the right look, either as Goth club-goers or as staff. The club management were aware of what was happening and had been very willing to help out. From what Conor could tell, his colleagues were well integrated into the crowd and doing a fantastic job of blending in. Neither he nor Alex showed any sign that they recognized anyone but it was reassuring to know that they were surrounded by people looking out for them.

The club was crowded, it was Saturday night after all, but Alex found a gap at the bar and nudged them a space. Conor schooled his expression into blandness and did his best to ignore the lewd comments directed at him. He endured the occasional grope and focused his attention on Alex in what he hoped was a suitably submissive way. Alex held him close, stroked his hair and occasionally kissed Conor's neck using his teeth more than his lips. Conor guessed that he was going to have several marks to show for the attention.

When the live band eventually came on to play, the majority of the crowd surged forward to get closer. Alex commandeered a couple of vacated stools, grabbed Conor from behind and lifted him onto one of them. Conor smiled sweetly and batted his lashes even though he wanted to punch the smug grin from Alex's face. His boss was enjoying his role far too much. Pressed close behind him Alex began to explore, slipping his hand beneath the hem of Conor's shirt and stroking his stomach. "I should put you in a collar more often, sweetheart. I don't want anyone thinking you're not claimed."

Conor jerked as Alex unfastened the buttons on his shirt and pulled it apart. In full view of anyone who cared to look Alex began to play with Conor's nipples, pinching and twisting each in turn. Plenty of people were watching and when Alex started to pull at the laces holding Conor's trousers closed, there was a collective hiss of indrawn breath. Conor closed his eyes and leaned back against the heat of Alex's body. Once he blanked out the fact that they were in a public place, surrounded by eager voyeurs and some of his colleagues, he could enjoy the sensation of Alex inserting his fingers beneath his filmy underwear. Conor was hard and aching. When Alex achieved his goal and Conor found his cock wrapped in a tight grip, he nearly came there and then.

"This is mine," Alex's voice was harsh. "Too many people are looking at you like you're available. You're not and you never will be. Nobody gets to touch you but me. Do you understand?"

Conor nodded frantically. "Yes, sir! I understand."

"So stop acting like a slut. Fuck, you're too pretty to take out, I should keep you locked up at home and I should keep this pretty prick confined to a cage."

"But I didn't do anything, sir!" Conor cringed as Alex squeezed harder, administering punishment.

Alex released Conor's cock but didn't redo his laces. He grabbed Conor's wrist in a bruising grip and pulled him into a dark corner where he shoved him back against the wall and kissed him violently. "Show me how sorry you are, slut, suck me!" Alex pushed down hard on Conor's shoulder, forcing him to his knees. Conor resisted, trying to push back, fighting hard.

"Stop! You're hurting me!"

"Shut the fuck up!" Alex slapped him hard across the face.

Conor shoved him away as firmly as he dared and staggered to his feet, yanking the laces on his trousers until they tightened and covered him. He ran for the door, roughly wiping away the tears that streaked his face. He turned briefly to see Alex shrug callously and return to the bar.

Conor grabbed his gear from the cloakroom and headed out into the dark. Pausing by the bike, he made a show of pulling himself together before mounting up. He took his time pulling on his gloves and fitting the snug helmet over his head, using the time to look around. He didn't spot anything suspicious as he kicked the bike stand up and moved away. His heart pounded but the drama with Alex was the cause of that—the scene they had planned had felt so real. He focused on the road and set off on the route home. Half of him hoped that nothing would happen—the other half prayed that it would.

Alex waited at the bar for as long as he could stand. He sipped his drink, gripping the glass far too hard. He sniffed at the liquid then looked up at the barman. "Can you smell burning?" An acrid smell of smoke lingered in the air.

"Yes. Bloody hell, something's on fire!" The barman turned and slammed his hand against the fire alarm, breaking the glass. The harsh jangling of a bell cut through the air. All the other noise faded as people gradually realized that the alarm was real. The smell of smoke got worse. The barman vaulted over the bar and began to usher club-goers toward the fire exits. Alex joined him, keeping people moving.

The side door was flung open and a rush of cold air signaled safety. Alex spilled outside in a wave of coughing, choking people. He held a handkerchief to his face and stopped to pull others free from the throng pushing at the narrow exit. Once he was satisfied that people were getting out easily enough, he moved toward the front of the club. Tiny flames licked beneath the main doors to The Black Orchid — malevolent little fingers of orange that appeared and disappeared in the narrow gap beneath the door. Puffs of black smoke squeezed through the crevices in the wood, seeping past hinges and joints, leaving smears of black residue on the paintwork.

A bouncer appeared at another exit. He was shouting and gesturing, "This way!" Along the road, a window exploded outwards, showering the pavement with glittering fragments of glass. Smoke billowed through the hole. Alarms screamed into the night and there was chaos as more and more people poured from the fire exits into the street.

Alex grabbed the nearest person he recognized. "Who's tracking Conor? I can't hear anything in this fucking racket!" He yanked out his useless earpiece that he'd inserted as soon as Conor had left him. It was supposed to be his communication channel with the van housing the tracking equipment. Officers were monitoring both the tracker in Conor's bracelet and the other one installed on the bike.

"I can't hear anything either, sir, it must be the smoke interfering with the receivers or something—I don't know how this techy shit works!"

Alex looked around, quickly assessing the situation. Though there was a lot of smoke, the flames seemed to have been restricted to just a few small areas inside the club. The street was full of people milling around in confusion and fire engine klaxons sounded in the distance.

"Check that no one's trapped inside, I'm going to the mobile unit."

He left his colleague attempting to impose some control on the crowd and sprinted down the street and around the corner to the mobile unit. He tore the van's rear doors open and yelled at the occupants, "Where is he?" Alex clambered into the van and squeezed himself into the narrow gap next to the tracking equipment.

"He's about three miles south of here. I have both his signals—he just stopped moving. What the hell's going on, sir, you stink of smoke?"

"The club's on fire."

"You've got to be fucking kidding me?" His colleague swore and fiddled with the equipment.

"No joke and it's just too fucking convenient a distraction. This has to have something to do with Rasputin." Alex held his breath, waiting for the little red light indicating Conor's location to start moving again. He had a sick feeling in the pit of his stomach. "Something's wrong, I'm going after him."

"Back-up car's parked in front of us—here." Alex caught the keys that his colleague tossed at him. "Wait! Take a headset so I can give you directions!" Alex shoved the wireless comms rig on and jumped from the back of the van, stumbling slightly in his haste. The lights on a black Audi flashed when he pressed the key remote. He dove into the driver's seat then fired up the vehicle. He pulled away with a squeal of rubber. He knew which route to take initially because Conor would have headed toward Alex's home.

The headset squawked in his ear, "Signal's still static. Head for the junction of Wilson Street and Main Road."

Alex drove as recklessly as he dared. The route was familiar and there was no traffic. Conor had headed the way they had planned and Alex knew where his destination was. It took him just a few minutes to reach the spot, but as he screeched to a halt he realized that he was still too late. He left the car skewed at an angle to the curb and jumped out. Conor's bike lay on its side in the middle of the road, shattered plastic from the rear reflectors glinting on the tarmac. Conor's helmet sat in the gutter, blood smearing the inside of the visor, but of Conor there was no sign. Alex's cry of rage, frustration and anguish echoed down the empty street. He sat down in the road, hugging Conor's helmet, barely aware of the frantic voice in his ear demanding information. Eventually he managed to respond, "He's gone. I've lost him." Whoever was on the other end of the radio cursed, "The tracker bracelet's stopped sending a signal as well. We've got nothing here. Damn it to hell."

For the first time in his life, Alex Courtney felt despair. It was as if someone had draped a black cloth over his senses — everything became dark and indistinct. He couldn't think, couldn't even breathe. The wail of sirens pierced his consciousness and he dragged in a ragged lungful of air. He realized that he was still sitting on the pavement clutching Conor's helmet like a security blanket. His arse was cold, his trousers soaked through from sitting on the wet ground. Shakily he got to his feet and went to greet his colleagues.

The road junction was rapidly roped off with crime scene tape. Within fifteen minutes the place swarmed with a scene of crime people. Flashes from cameras and the rotating blue of panda car lights lit up the scene like the interior of a nightclub until floodlights were erected and turned night into day. Alex handed over Conor's helmet and accepted the disapproving look from the crime scene tech because he'd daubed fingerprints all over it. The juvenile error snapped him out of the daze he was in. He wouldn't be any help to Conor if he made stupid mistakes. Alex's priority was to find Conor, as quickly as possible. He needed him home, safely tucked up in bed where he belonged.

"Guv! Over here!"

Alex looked up to see Higgs waving at him from behind the tape, two mugs of something hot balanced in one hand.

"Trust you to think tea will make everything better." Alex grabbed one of the mugs and wrapped his chilled fingers around its comforting warmth.

"Tea does make everything better. It's a well-known fact. And the crime scene lads never travel anywhere without a decent brew on hand." Higgs blew on his own drink and took a noisy slurp. "Well, this all went to hell in a handcart, didn't it?"

"That's it, Higgs, cushion the blow, why don't you?"

Higgs shrugged. "Nothing I can say is going to make this any better. I've recalled the team to the office. They'll be ready and waiting to do whatever needs to be done to get our boy back."

Alex smiled grimly. To Higgs, Conor was still a boy and Alex took no offense at the older man's use of the word. Higgs occasionally referred to Alex in the same way. Higgs knew when to be deferential but most of the time he spoke as he saw. It was refreshing.

Alex swallowed his tea and thumped the mug down on the nearest wall. "You're right, of course. Do you know what's going on at The Black Orchid? Was anyone hurt in the fire?"

"Everybody got out. Couple of people were carted off by the paramedics suffering from smoke inhalation, but nothing serious. All our people were good. I spoke to the fire boys while I was there. An accelerant was used — some kind of chemical had been sprayed along the window sills and at the base of the main doors — the ones that aren't used."

"It was a deliberate distraction." Alex rolled his shoulders. "We've underestimated Rasputin. We assumed that he selected and watched his victims, but thought that he took them opportunistically. We were wrong. This was carefully planned."

Higgs nodded. "The bastard's got some nerve, that's for sure."

Alex paced up and down. "He must have known this was a trap. We've never hidden the fact that Conor and I are policemen and he isn't stupid. We gave him a tempting target and he took it. Setting the fire bought him some time, but not much. He would have known that we would be after Conor as soon as we got out of there, that's why he took him down so quickly. We're only three miles from the club."

Higgs leaned against the wall. "Do you think he has an accomplice? How could he start the fire and intercept Conor? There wouldn't be enough time."

"We've never found any evidence that someone else is involved in the murders. It's possible, I suppose, but maybe he used some kind of remote device to start the blaze? Hopefully the fire boys will turn something up, they're the experts. I don't know, Higgs, my gut says this guy's a loner. I don't think he'd want to share his victims, but that's just my instincts at work, nothing concrete."

"Well, your gut is usually a pretty good judge of character, boss, and for what it's worth, I'm inclined to agree."

Alex waved at the supervising crime scene officer. "Arnie, what have you got? Anything useful yet?"

"Fuck, Alex, it's been less than an hour," Arnie said impatiently. "Still, I know this involves one of yours so I'll risk a few educated guesses." He paused and surveyed the scene. "There's no sign that another vehicle was involved in the accident. We haven't found any paint on the bike and there's no debris in the road other than that from the bike. That's the first thing."

Alex and Higgs looked at one another. That was good.

Less chance that Conor had been seriously hurt.

"Your man went over and slid the length of the junction. There are scrapings of leather on the tarmac. The blood in the helmet looks dramatic but there isn't that much there, it could have come from a small cut—maybe from his lip as it's about the right place to be level with his mouth. The bad news is that it looks like the helmet hit the curb and that's how he came to a stop. If he hit hard enough, he may have lost consciousness. We haven't had time to calculate how fast he was going yet."

"Fuck." Alex kicked an innocent piece of gravel along the pavement.

"The lad's got a hard head, guv, don't worry."

"What else, Arnie?"

"The two CCTV cameras that cover this junction have had their lenses spray painted over and two of the three lamp posts have been vandalized. You're going to have to look at a wide area to find footage of possible vehicles because there aren't any more cameras in this neighborhood."

"He's doing everything he can to slow us down." A sharp pain throbbed at Alex's temple.

"We do have one possible witness."

"What? Arnie, why the fuck did you leave that little fact till last?" Alex wanted to get hold of the other man and shake some sense into him.

Higgs drew Arnie to one side. "Spill it before the boss decks you."

Arnie edged nervously away. "Yes, right. There's a chap lives up the street over there"—he gestured to the road on the north side of the junction—"an old bloke—got curious when he heard the sirens and wandered down here in his dressing gown and slippers. He says there was a white van parked outside his house when he went to bed at about eleven. Doesn't know whether it was there earlier but it wasn't a vehicle he recognized. He got a couple of letters from the registration plate—he couldn't see the rest from the angle it was at. He also said it had a sliding door on

150

the side rather than doors at the back. No windows that he noticed and no insignia. Couldn't tell us the make."

"That should help with the CCTV footage if nothing else. Something to look out for. Thanks, Arnie. If you come up with anything else, you know how to get hold of us." Higgs gave him a pat on the shoulder.

"Hope it works out." Arnie walked back to his crew.

"I don't think there's much use in us staying here, boss, let's get back to the station and regroup."

Alex sighed heavily. "Sure, and thanks for preventing the GBH I was about to commit on Arnie. It's not his fault he's an idiot, he was born that way."

Higgs snorted. "Come on, we've got work to do."

Chapter Twelve

Conor knew he was cold, but he couldn't work out why. He'd been dreaming—vague images of ice and fire. He tried to grab hold of a picture and bring it into focus but it remained blurry and out of reach. *Dreaming, just dreaming.* He attempted to pull himself into the real world. It was dark, much darker than Alex's bedroom and, oh God, his head hurt like the devil. Had he been drinking? He didn't drink, though, never had—he hated the taste of alcohol. Maybe someone had spiked his drink at the club—could you spike water without it tasting strange? He wasn't sure about that.

Gradually his muddled brain began to make sense of his surroundings. There was cold stone beneath him—it was dry and smooth but dusty. Little gritty grains irritated his fingertips. So he was inside a building because this wasn't tarmac. Why would it be tarmac? Conor groaned as it all came back to him—the bike, riding away from The Black Orchid, away from Alex. He'd come to a junction and the street lamps had been broken. Just as he'd pulled away a van had shot out in front of him, no lights, no warning. He'd swerved to avoid it but the road had been wet. He'd lost control and had gone down.

He remembered his shoulder hitting the ground, sliding along with the bike's weight pinning him down, a sharp pain in his knee, then nothing. From the jackhammer pounding inside his head his slide must have been arrested by something solid. But how had he gotten here, to this place? He groped for understanding through pain that made it difficult to think. His helmet was gone and apparently his jacket and shirt too because the stone chilled his upper body. He tried to sit up but couldn't. What the hell was wrong with his arms? Was he injured? He couldn't move them. He wriggled a shoulder and winced at renewed pain, then proceeded to test each joint with the tiniest of movements. By the time he got to his wrists he realized that nothing was broken but that his hands were tied behind his back. No, not tied, chained. Metal dug into the flesh of his wrists and it clinked as he moved. The restraints were heavier, wider than handcuffs, the metal rough against his skin. He bent his fingers, trying to feel. He closed his eyes and concentrated on the small task, pushing back the growing feeling of panic that gnawed at his guts. The cuffs were about two inches wide and thick, joined by only two links of chain. They were made of iron rather than steel because they were heavy, and he could just make out the shape of a keyhole. They were old-fashioned manacles of some kind.

Making a heroic effort, Conor managed to lever his body into a sitting position and shuffled backwards on his arse until he could lean against a wall. Even that small amount of movement was exhausting. His eyes gradually adjusted to the darkness but he could only make out the vague shape of a door on the other side of the room. The tiniest sliver of light gave it an outline. He took a few slow breaths. The pain in his head was making him feel nauseated and the last thing he wanted to do was throw up.

Once the urge to vomit had subsided, Conor attempted to assess his condition as clinically as possible. His feet were bare and heavy shackles chafed his ankles. *Probably part of a nice matching set.* He was still wearing the laced leather trousers that he'd had on at the club, but that was all. He shivered and did a mental inventory of the injuries he could feel. His face was sticky on one side—it felt like partially dried blood, presumably from whatever wound was making his head throb. His lip was split because when he licked at it, it stung. His shoulder felt stiff and sore, and he knew that it had taken the brunt of the impact when the bike had gone down. Hopefully his leather jacket had prevented too much damage. His knee was the worst. Conor had a pretty high tolerance for pain but it felt like someone had drilled a hole above his knee. It hurt in exactly the same place as before when he'd ripped the ligaments above his knee. It had taken several months of intensive and painful physiotherapy to recover from that injury and now it felt like he was going to have to go through the whole agonizing process again.

"I think I'm in trouble," he muttered to himself then gave a slightly hysterical chuckle. He had no idea how long he'd been unconscious or even if it were night or day. Since meeting Alex he'd had a few interesting dreams involving chains, but this was a very long way from his fantasies. This was a nightmare brought to life. He wanted to deny it but deep down he knew that Rasputin had to be responsible for his current predicament. The fact that no one seemed to be battering down the door to rescue him meant that his kidnapping had been well planned and executed. He wondered idly if Rasputin would turn out to be one of the suspects he had identified. It would be nice to be right. If he had to make a guess, he would go with Bates. The man was clever and manipulative—a much more likely candidate to have pulled this off than Leary.

A small seed of worry for Alex began to germinate in Conor's mind. Something must have prevented him from giving chase and Conor knew that it would have to have been pretty serious. Alex would have done anything to keep him safe. If Rasputin were clever enough to take Conor without being caught then he would definitely have considered how to remove Alex from the equation. "Please let him be okay," Conor whispered. Hurt and trapped though he was, Alex's well-being was more important than his own plight. He couldn't stand the thought that his lover might be hurt or worse.

His lover. Maybe it was finally time to admit that he

loved Alex. His feelings were so strong, how could they be anything else? In the darkness Conor smiled. Perhaps he really was in love for the very first time. He wondered if he would ever get the chance to tell Alex how he felt. Did Alex feel the same? He'd never said so. There had been moments when something had seemed to break through the icy façade that Alex cultivated most of the time. Little hints that maybe, just maybe he felt something deeper than lust. Conor was too inexperienced to know for sure and he didn't want to blurt out his feelings only to discover that Alex didn't return them. Best to just enjoy what they had rather than risk spoiling things with mushy emotions. *For fuck's sake! I can't believe I'm sat here, chained up in some maniac's private dungeon, giving myself relationship advice. What the hell is wrong with me? Stress. It must be stress.* Conor giggled hysterically. It was better than crying.

Despite the cold and discomfort Conor drifted into an uneasy sleep. When he awoke he was still alone. He knew that hours had passed because he was hungry, thirsty and his arms ached. Where the hell was the cavalry? Surely the tracker bracelet was sending his location back to some tech wizard at the station. His whole body was sore but the throbbing in his head had subsided a little. He really should attempt to get up and explore his prison, though he doubted that Rasputin would have missed an escape route. Conor bent his uninjured knee and pressed back against the wall. Using his hands he gradually pushed himself up the stonework until he was standing, albeit precariously.

He used the wall as support and edged around the room. Reaching a corner was a milestone. Conor also felt like he'd run a marathon. At least he wasn't cold anymore. Sweat stung his damaged shoulder and trickled down his bare chest. All he'd managed to achieve were some new scrapes on his back and the knowledge that his cell was at least eight feet across. He turned the corner and began the painful shuffle along the next wall. If nothing else it gave him an aim. A goal to work toward.

A small red light blinked above the door. It definitely hadn't been there before, there was no way he would have missed it. Conor edged toward it as quickly as he could manage. It was hard to see anything in the gloom but he could just make out the reflection of a round lens. Conor glared and mouthed *fuck you* in the direction of the light.

Seconds later, the red light clicked off. Conor pressed back against the wall even though he knew it provided no protection. He needed something solid behind him to hold him up. Heavy footsteps sounded outside the door, the noise echoing as if in a tunnel, getting closer. A key scraped in a lock and the heavy door swung open with a creak. Conor blinked into the brightness that filled the doorway. A figure, silhouetted against the light, stepped forwards and Conor got his first look at a serial killer.

He was short and stocky, wearing workman's boots and blue coveralls topped by a ripped, hooded sweatshirt. The hood was pulled up, covering his head and concealing his face in shadows. In his hand was an enormous hunting knife, the blade glinting wickedly. Conor found his eyes drawn to the weapon—images of what it had done flashed through his mind with horrifying clarity.

"My, my—you are definitely the prettiest so far, if not especially polite." The voice was raspy and higher than Conor had expected. "I'm glad I kept you. We are going to have such fun together."

Conor swallowed. What the hell did you say to a mad man brandishing a knife that looked like it could take down a rampaging grizzly bear?

"You need help. Let me go and I'll make sure you get it." It took all Conor's will to stop his voice from shaking. He tried to remember everything he'd ever been taught about negotiation. Unfortunately the police college didn't have an extensive series of lectures that covered being held at knifepoint by a psychopathic maniac.

"Oh, I don't think there's any going back now, do you?" Rasputin took a couple of steps into the room and closed the gap between them. The knife dangled from his fingers.

"You can't undo what you've done, but you don't have to hurt me too." Conor kept his tone even and reasonable. Rasputin pushed his hood back and revealed his face. He was utterly nondescript, with the kind of face that would never be noticed in a crowd. Neither ugly nor handsome, his features were uniformly plain. Conor felt a tiny measure of satisfaction that his work had paid off when he recognized the man from his picture in the incident room. Rasputin was Cyril Bates. The only things that stood out were his eyes. They were dead. Dark and lifeless, there wasn't even a hint of light in their cold depths. Bates smiled – his look of satisfaction sent a shard of ice into Conor's heart. He knew madness when he saw it. There would be no negotiating with this man – his only chance of survival was to buy as much time as he could and pray that Alex found him.

Bates held out the knife and gestured at the door. "If you promise to be good I'll take you to a bathroom and clean up that head wound."

Conor had no idea why Rasputin would want to clean him up before killing him, but what the hell? He nodded and stepped away from the wall. Rasputin moved behind him, pressed the point of the blade into his neck and unlocked the manacles from one wrist.

"Lock them again – in front of you." He pressed home his point with the knife and a trickle of blood slid down Conor's neck. Conor squeezed the cuff shut – at least it was slightly more comfortable this way round, though his arm muscles burned at the sudden change of position. What worried him more was the battered tracker bracelet that sat just above the cuff. It looked like someone had taken a hammer to it and the deep grazes on his skin attested to the battering that side of his body had taken when he'd come off the bike.

"Your chains are interesting, are they not? A little piece of history that I obtained from a museum that was closing down its slavery exhibition. So much more substantial than the modern versions. You really can get anything on eBay these days." Bates' tone was frighteningly conversational. "You first." The sting of the knife prodded him forward into the yellow light of the corridor. Bare feet and chains made for slow progress, but Conor's knee was on fire, so he was grateful he could only limp along. Bates didn't rush him but reminded him of the knife with a little jab every now and again.

Flickering fluorescent tubes strung along a makeshift wire lit the corridor. Light green paint peeled away from the walls. Doors with small windows appeared at intervals but Conor couldn't make out anything through the filthy glass as he hobbled by. The bathroom they eventually reached was institutional — there were rectangular white tiles from floor to ceiling, cracked and covered in thick grime. A rat scurried the length of the urinal trough, its little beady eyes communicating annoyance at being disturbed.

"I imagine you need to go. I wouldn't want you feeling uncomfortable while we play, so please avail yourself of the facilities." Bates giggled as if he'd just made a prize-winning joke. Realizing that the crazy man was actually right, Conor shuffled into a stall. He struggled with the fastenings on his trousers and eventually managed to relieve himself. He struggled to tie the laces up again but managed a loose knot. Bates hummed behind him, something that sounded suspiciously like a Kylie Minogue song. Conor decided that fate would not be so unkind as to let him die to such a hideous soundtrack. There had to be some hope.

Bates nudged him toward the sink. The ancient mirror above it was cracked and mottled with black patches but there was enough clear surface for Conor to be shocked at his own reflection. One side of his face was caked with dried blood from a hairline tear in his skin. His shoulder was black with bruising and raw with road rash, though his jacket must have saved him from worse damage. His skin was even whiter than usual and dark circles like bruises shadowed his eyes.

Conor didn't expect the taps to work but when Bates turned the faucet on, brown liquid gushed out in a sputtering stream.

"Clean yourself up." Bates handed him a rag that might once have been a handkerchief. Conor held it under the water until it was soaked through then dabbed at his face, softening the congealed blood. He tried to ignore the malevolent presence beside him and played for time as he washed.

"Do you have a name? I can't call you Rasputin."

The knife twirled in podgy fingers. "Bates. But I think you already knew that, Detective."

Conor gripped the sink hard.

Bates cackled merrily. "Oh yes, I know what you are. You and your tall blond friend—not my type, by the way, but I can see why you went for him. You were getting close, weren't you? Dangled the bait in front of me like a wriggly worm. Well, I took it, didn't I? But you didn't hook me! I love games. Such fun."

Conor stared at Bates in the mirror.

"The inspector should treat you better, though. He doesn't deserve you. You're much better off with me. Still, the little fire I arranged should have dealt with him. He won't be around to bother you anymore. He was starting to get annoying anyway. I was thinking of moving on and plying my trade somewhere else."

"Fire? What fire? What have you done?"

Bates crowed his delight. "He'll be fried and crispy, not nearly so handsome with his face gone." Anger surged through Conor. He swung his cuffed arms hard toward Bates and made satisfying contact with his smug face, but before he could celebrate, a heavy boot slammed into his injured knee and he collapsed to the ground. Conor curled on the floor trying to protect himself as Bates kicked at him in a frenzy.

"Now that was very naughty." Bates spat blood and the spray misted across Conor's chest. "And naughty boys must be punished, don't you agree?" Bates wrapped a fist in Conor's hair and dragged him to his feet.

Conor sobbed as he was pushed and shoved back to his prison. He fell twice, the second time almost blacking out as white agony flashed across his vision.

"You need to learn some manners. That boyfriend of yours obviously didn't spank your pretty arse enough."

Exhausted, Conor sprawled on the floor when Bates shoved him down. Now that the room was lighter Conor could see the heavy hook dangling from a chain pulley system fixed to the ceiling. Bates fiddled with it until he could lower the hook almost to the floor. He looped the chain from Conor's manacles around the hook then used the pulley rope to haul him to his feet. Conor screamed as he was yanked upright until his arms were stretched taut, his toes only just scraping the floor. All his weight was suspended from his wrists and blood dripped slowly down his arms as the metal cuffs bit into his flesh.

Bates circled him, laughing. His eyes were wild, drool spilling from his mouth. "Now you just wait here a while and think about what a bad boy you've been. I'll be back shortly, promise." That wasn't the kind of promise that Conor wanted to hear but it gave him a few moments' respite. This insufferable little man that the press had turned into a walking nightmare had taken the lives of four innocent young men. He hadn't made any attempt to justify his actions. Conor cursed under his breath. He would not give Bates the satisfaction of showing fear. Pain meant he was alive. "Hurry, Alex, please hurry," he whispered, the words laced with blood.

"He's not coming for you, pretty, I told you." Bates was back, all too soon. He peered up at Conor. "You're mine now and it's time to play." He spread an immaculate white cloth on the floor at Conor's feet and laid out a set of pristine knives in varying sizes.

"I think you could at least tell me why?" Conor whispered, his throat aching and sore.

"Why not?"

"How can you say that? What gives you the right to take life? What makes you so special?" Conor spat the words at his tormentor.

Bates tilted his head to one side. "Have you ever let your lover shove his cock so far down your throat that he controls your breathing? Have you ever let him mark you? Make you bleed? I just take the final step. I provide the ultimate ecstasy. That's not wrong."

Bates picked up a small knife, circled behind Conor then hacked at his hair until Conor's short ponytail fell to the floor. He returned to where Conor could see him and set the knife down, picking up another that was more like a scalpel. "It's important to use the correct tool for each job, don't you agree?" He set the point against the laces fastening Conor's trousers and sliced each lace. The ties parted and the leather separated. Conor thrashed against his restraints but could do nothing to stop Bates cutting through the thin layer of his underwear, exposing his cock. Bates giggled and stroked Conor's flaccid dick. "I'll save that for later, when you are a bit more cooperative." He swapped knives again, laying the scalpel gently back on the cloth and picking up a blade that curved at the end like an oriental dagger. *I should be so lucky, lucky, lucky, lucky...* Bates sang tunelessly. He made patterns in the air with the knife then placed the point of the blade against Conor's chest and delicately drew it across his skin.

Chapter Thirteen

Alex tried to repress the waves of panic that repeatedly threatened to drown his ability to think clearly. His gut churned and his throat was dry, he wanted to scream and shout and break things. Twenty-six hours had passed since Conor had been taken. The longest, most soul destroying hours he had ever experienced.

It was three o'clock in the morning and Alex hadn't slept or eaten. There was no way he was going to waste time with either when he could be searching for the only man who had meant anything to him in a very long time. He was surviving on adrenaline and strong coffee as he and his team went over and over everything they knew about Rasputin. It wasn't much.

Of the three suspects that Conor had identified, one had already been discounted. Neither of the others had been spotted at The Black Orchid, but that didn't mean that they hadn't been there. Alex had people going through reams of CCTV footage from every working camera within a five-mile radius of the club. Uniformed police were questioning everyone that had been at The Black Orchid, showing them pictures of the two suspects. Higgs was going back over all of Conor's notes and scanning the case files from the beginning. It all had to be done but it took time and that was something they didn't have.

Alex knew that all of Rasputin's previous victims had been killed within twelve hours of being taken. He paced and muttered and dragged his fingers through his hair until he looked like an agitated blond hedgehog.

Higgs shoved another cup of steaming black coffee into

his hand. "I'm not going to tell you to go home or sleep, boss, because I know that would be pointless, but at least sit down before you fall down. The first aid kit contains an ancient crêpe bandage, two sticking plasters and some insect repellent. If you damage yourself, there'll be nothing I can do for you."

Alex summoned a small smile. "You'd make someone a good mother, Higgs." He collapsed into a chair. "We're missing something, I know we are. Something obvious. No killer completely disappears." He slammed the coffee down on the nearest surface, slopping it everywhere. "The bracelet! Why would it stop working? It's a sealed unit. Why would we not be able to receive the signal?" As far as they knew, Conor's tracker bracelet had not been removed. It certainly hadn't been found at the scene of the bike accident or in any of the surrounding streets. Of course it was possible that it had been cut off and lobbed down a drain or thrown into a hedge, but why would Rasputin suspect a piece of jewelry was anything other that what it appeared to be?

"Hate to be negative but it could have been damaged in the accident," Higgs said glumly.

One of the others piped up, "What about interference or shielding of some kind?"

"Like what? You know I'm a technical idiot, Phil, what might have that effect?" Alex stood and began moving around again. Sitting still just didn't feel right. He had to be on the go — to feel like he was doing something constructive.

"Well, lead or a heavy metal. Somewhere underground. Maybe even somewhere near a telecommunications mast or something like that. Any of those things might affect it, it didn't have a particularly long range, did it?" Alex frowned, "No — we never expected him to get very far away from us. But it's something to look at. Check maps of the area for anything that might jam the signal — masts, electronic installations, underground storage... And focus on the area around the hospital. I have a hunch that Conor's link is important." He turned to Higgs. "Don't know why, though."

"Hey, there's a lot to be said for instinct. Your guts helped us out before." Higgs patted his own ample middle. "Of course, if you were a bit better padded, your gut might be more reliable."

Alex snorted and gave Higgs a wry smile. He knew what the gruff sergeant was trying to do and, strangely, his humor did calm Alex a little. He watched the flurry of activity and paper shuffling going on around him as maps and plans of the city were examined and discarded.

"Here, boss! This could be it!" Phil dashed across the room, a large sheet of paper flapping wildly in his hand. Blueprints of the hospital were thrust under Alex's nose. "Slow down, Phil! I can't see anything with you doing origami on speed!" Alex grabbed the plans and smoothed them down on a table. They looked like so many lines and blue squiggling to him.

Phil banged the table. "You might not remember, but I grew up here. The current hospital was built on the site of an old Victorian asylum. It was a massive place, really spooky. As kids we used to dare each other to go inside the abandoned buildings, make up horror stories about it, that kind of thing."

"Phil, I don't need your life history. We all know you were a complete wuss as a kid."

"Yeah, yeah... Tease the guy who's trying to tell you something. Look, when the asylum was demolished they built on top of the original basement. It was converted to what's now the morgue. It was a money-saving thing, you know—not having to redo the foundations."

Alex nodded. "I know it. I've been down to the morgue a few times."

"Sure, haven't we all?" Higgs grinned. "It's one of my favorite spots for a lunch break. Nice and quiet."

"Jesus!" Phil thumped Higgs' shoulder. "Look! Compare the plans of the asylum with the new building. They don't match. The old basement extends beyond where the new building finishes. There must still be rooms underground there somewhere."

Alex stared at the diagrams.

"There's more," Phil carried on, the pitch of his voice rising. "The ground above that area was sold off to raise money to help fund the new hospital. It was sold to a mobile phone company — there's a telecommunications mast right on top of it."

Alex was already moving. "Let's go. There are too many coincidences here to ignore. If this is where Rasputin is killing, the whole hospital link makes sense. Bates and Leary would both have had the opportunity to investigate and explore, maybe find the abandoned rooms. Phil, stay here. Call the hospital and the mobile phone company. I know it's early, but wake people up. I don't care who you have to piss off. Talk to the fire boys at The Black Orchid again, see if they've got anything new for us. Keep in touch." Phil didn't answer, just picked up the nearest phone and started stabbing at the buttons.

Alex headed for the door, Higgs and the rest of his team close behind him. It felt good to be taking action. He pushed thoughts of what Conor might be going through to the back of his mind. Conor was strong and knew what he was doing. He'd been in difficult situations before. If anyone could survive a killer, it was him.

As they drove across town at breakneck speed, Alex kept catching glimpses of the enormous telecommunications mast towering above the skyline. He wondered why he'd never really noticed it before. It just merged into the background, anonymous and unimportant. It made him think about their suspects. He'd bet his salary that Bates was the killer. He was as anonymous as the mast, blending into the background. An invisible man. Leary was far more visible, violent and arrogant. Rasputin was clever enough to have killed four times without being caught. He was a shadowy figure in a hood, nothing more.

They got to the base of the mast in less than ten minutes. A twelve-foot fence topped with razor wire surrounded it. A single gate was set into the fence, locked with an enormous padlock and chain. Alex took one look and cursed. "Don't panic, guv, a good policeman is always equipped." Higgs went to the boot of the car and liberated a set of heavy-duty bolt cutters. He made short work of the gate and they were in.

Alex gave his sergeant a hard look. "Do I need to ask what else you have hidden in the car, Higgs?"

"Best you don't." Higgs winked.

Alex shrugged. He had more important things to worry about than whether or not his sergeant was engaging in a bit of breaking and entering on the side. Like how the hell they were supposed to access the abandoned basement. It was dark, and though they had torches, there was no obvious way in. The mast was built on a concrete platform and the area around it was covered in long, scrubby grass and weeds. Brambles tangled with nettles in a fight for the prize of most irritating plant life. Alex kicked at a particularly thorny creeper that seemed to have an attraction to his trouser leg and succeeded only in scratching his calf. He ripped his leg away and stumbled. Something clanged beneath his foot.

"Over here!" Alex yelled as he kicked at the weeds around his feet. Higgs used the bolt cutters to clear the brambles and finally a metal manhole cover was revealed. Alex sighed. "If Rasputin is here, he's using a different access point. Those brambles haven't been moved recently."

"Doesn't mean anything, boss, don't give up." Higgs was clearly a mind reader. Alex shook his head. His sergeant was right, they had to keep going. He got to his knees, ignoring the stab of thorns, and helped to lever up the metal cover. It fell back with a loud clang and Alex winced, hoping that they hadn't just announced their presence to anyone below. Underneath, a ladder descended into the darkness. Alex stamped on the top rung, testing its strength. The rusty metal creaked but didn't give way.

"I'll go first." Alex grinned at Higgs in an obvious attempt to disguise his fear. "Your weight might be too much of a challenge for this metalwork, Higgs."

Higgs grinned right back. "Cheeky whelp. If you weren't my boss I'd give you a clip round the ear!"

Alex swung himself onto the rickety ladder and descended into the darkness, Higgs and two uniformed policemen close behind him. He hit the bottom of the shaft and his feet sank into three inches of accumulated muck. In the dim light he could just about see the walls of the small concrete bunker he was standing in, which was less than ten feet across. Opposite him was a rusting access panel. The space began to get crowded as his colleagues joined him so he moved to the door and gingerly tested the handle. Rust ground into his palm but there was a small amount of movement. "What I wouldn't give for a can of WD-40," he muttered. "Fuck, Higgs, this is going to make a noise and we've no idea what's behind here. What if we push Rasputin into doing something stupid?"

"Chance we have to take I think, guv."

Alex nodded and applied his strength to the door handle. The resulting squeal was worse than the sound of nails dragging down a blackboard and it echoed around the small area, making Alex cringe. But the door was open. The hinges grated as he pushed it wide and stepped through into a broad corridor. In the distance lights flickered.

Alex made room for the others and gestured for quiet, pointing at the illumination ahead of them. "Looks like we've struck the jackpot and our killer's not expecting visitors," Alex whispered. "He's complacent. That's good." He pushed down his feelings of dread at what they might find and moved silently along the passage. As they got closer to the glow, they heard singing. There was an open door in the distance, a square of light outlined on the corridor floor. Alex started to run. He skidded to a halt in the patch of brightness and turned through the door into a scene from a horror film.

Rasputin was in a world of his own, dancing in Conor's blood and waving a knife like a conductor's baton. Conor hung from chains, semi-naked, his chest streaked scarlet. There was no way of knowing if he was alive. Time slowed as Alex met the crazed eyes of a killer. Thoughts flashed through his head — *It's Bates, we were right! He's insane. He hurt the man I love — Conor — need to get Conor away from here.* Rasputin's eyes were cold. Cackling, he raised the knife and plunged it toward Conor's chest. Alex threw himself between Conor and the weapon. He caught Rasputin's wrist as his arm came down and squeezed hard, grinding the bones together. The blade nicked Alex's cheek as it flew into the air, released from Rasputin's grasp.

Higgs and the others surged past and took Rasputin to the ground, pinning him down. The knife skittered away to rest against the wall. For a few seconds Alex could only stare at the stained blade. Ignoring the struggling pile of bodies on the floor, he ran to his lover, frantically looking for a way to release the chains. To his utter amazement, Conor's dark head lifted. His green eyes were dulled by pain but he managed the hint of a smile. In a barely audible voice he whispered, "Nice timing." Then his eyes rolled back in his head and he lost consciousness.

"I gave him what you never will," Rasputin shouted back as he was dragged away. "I'll haunt his dreams... He'll never be yours again." The words barely registered as Alex lowered Conor gently to the floor and cradled him in his arms.

* * * *

Conor felt warm and safe, drifting in a comfortable haze. Flashes of a nightmare began to upset his relaxed lassitude. It was like someone was jabbing little pinholes in a black piece of paper, allowing tiny beams of bright light through. It was unsettling and vague feelings of anxiety made his muscles tense. That brought pain, a dull aching throb that permeated every bone and tendon. Gradually he forced his eyes open, his breath coming in short, panicked gasps.

"Hey! It's all right, Conor. I'm here. Just relax, okay? You're in the hospital."

"Alex." Everything was going to be all right. Alex was with him. Conor's vision swam slowly into focus and the first things he saw were Alex's anxious eyes. His fingers were squeezed then Alex kissed him gently. The pain faded into the background.

"Not dead then?"

Conor's throat felt like sandpaper. "Not quite."

A cup of ice chips was held to his lips and the sensation as they melted on his tongue was heavenly.

"I'm so sorry, Conor." Alex's voice shook.

"For what?"

"Taking so long to find you."

"Don't... I," Conor whimpered as images of what he'd been through flashed into his head. He didn't move. He didn't want to discover that Alex was just a dream and that he was still chained, feeling the kiss of Rasputin's knife.

He cringed as someone touched his hair. He didn't dare look, but Alex's soothing voice followed, "You're safe, I promise."

Conor shuddered and he could do nothing to prevent the tears that rolled down his face. Exhausted, he slipped into darkness.

When he woke again a few hours later, Alex was gone. Conor tried to sit up, fighting the lines attached to his body. The door to his room swung open and Alex was back, clutching a paper cup of something hot.

"It's all right! I'm here. Keep still, you idiot!" He put the cup on the bedside cupboard unit and pushed Conor gently down.

Conor sank back against his pillows. "Idiot? What happened to cosseting the invalid?"

"This particular invalid is going to get his arse smacked if he tries to get up before the doc says it's okay."

Conor looked up at Alex who stood with his arms crossed.

"Promises, promises." Conor laughed weakly. "Your bedside manner stinks."

"I know. I hate hospitals, sorry. Can I get you anything?"

"Just some water please." Conor took the cup Alex offered him and sipped slowly before looking up. "You look tired." That was an understatement. Alex look exhausted, with black rings under his eyes and a couple of days' worth of golden stubble.

Alex chuckled and rubbed at his chin. "You've given me a couple of sleepless nights recently, and for all the wrong reasons."

"I'm sorry I was such a mess when I woke up earlier. I just wasn't sure what was real. Drugs I suppose."

Alex's lips quirked. "I think you were entitled to get a bit emotional and you have enough narcotics floating in your system to keep you happy for quite a while."

Conor looked down, not wanting to meet Alex's penetrating gaze. "Did you get him? Bates?"

"We did. He's securely under lock and key, don't worry. You were right, Conor."

"He told me you were gone, that he'd set a fire..." Conor almost choked on the words.

"He did. We're still not entirely sure how he managed it, but The Black Orchid is no more. Everyone got out, though. Death by fire wasn't his style. He wasn't interested in anyone in the club, he was just making sure that he could get to you without interference." Alex retrieved his drink and perched on the edge of the bed, smoothing the covers with his free hand.

"Alex, I..." Conor hesitated. "When he started...cutting me, I closed my eyes and you were there. I saw your face and I could bear the agony."

Gentle fingers touched his cheek and turned his head. Ice blue eyes gazed down at him, liquid with tears. "When I thought I'd lost you it was more than I could stand. I thought the pain would tear me apart." Alex kissed him. "Can you forgive me?"

"There's nothing to forgive." Conor didn't understand what Alex was getting at.

"I put you in terrible danger. You could have died. The operation went to pieces..." Alex stood up and paced, his agitation apparent in every step.

"Typical! Still ignoring the fact that I'm a grown-up. When I agreed to be part of this I knew exactly what I was getting into, Alex. You can't protect me all the time. The only guilty person in this whole mess is Bates. Give yourself a break."

Alex dumped his cup in the bin and returned to the bed. "Are you telling me what to do again?"

Conor blinked. He might be hurt but he wasn't immune to Alex's sexy growl. "Maybe."

Alex shook his head. "Just wait till you're better. You need to rest, to heal. Close your eyes. I'm here and I'm not going anywhere."

"I don't want to sleep, I want to go home. When can I get out of here?" Conor felt a bit belligerent, he didn't like being helpless.

"You were dehydrated and you've lost quite a lot of blood, so you need to stay on the drip for the next twelve hours at least, maybe longer. The doc stitched your head wound because it was a bit ragged and she cleaned your shoulder up. That was mainly grazing."

Conor tried to look at the bandages. "I don't remember anything about the bike going down. I woke up in that room that Bates had me in. I don't even know where I was."

"An abandoned basement of the old asylum underneath the new hospital."

"An asylum—how apt, if somewhat cliché," Conor muttered.

"Thankfully the cuts on your chest are shallow. They're taped up but you'll need to keep still while they knit a little. Your wrists are cut and bruised from the chains and you have some damage to the ligaments above your knee. I think they'll let you out tomorrow, if you promise to take it easy."

Conor sighed. "Why don't you go home and get some rest then. I'll be fine and you look shattered."

Alex scowled. "I said I was staying and I meant it. You really need to learn to stop arguing with me, but we'll save that discussion for a time when you are better able to deal with the consequences." He entwined his fingers with Conor's.

"I'll look forward to that." Conor's eyelids drooped again. He squeezed Alex's hand tightly. "Thanks for being here." He knew he should let go but Alex's touch was as good as a security blanket. Conor gave himself up to sleep again. He didn't fight it – the sooner he was rested, the sooner he and Alex could go home.

Chapter Fourteen

It was closer to two days before Conor's doctor was satisfied that the cuts on his chest would not reopen if he moved around. After what seemed like an interminable amount of poking and prodding, and a mountain of paperwork, he was finally released. Conor had to wait for Alex to come back — he'd eventually relented and taken a few hours to sleep, let Agnes know that they were both alive and well and check in at the station. When Alex finally pushed his way past the nurses who seemed to permanently hover around, Conor was prepared to climb out of the window in order to escape.

"At last! Please, Alex, break me out of here before I need a padded cell next door to Bates!"

Alex laughed and turned to the nurses. "Ladies. Much as I enjoy your delightful company, Detective Trethuan needs to get dressed, so perhaps you could give us some privacy?"

Neither of the young women looked like they had any intention of moving. Alex looked at them expectantly.

"Oh, you mean us? Are you sure you don't need some help, Inspector? We're very highly trained." One of them giggled.

Alex ushered them both from the room and shut the door firmly. "Little minxes. They just want to ogle your hot body."

Conor's face heated. "And you don't?" He unfastened the ties on the drawstring scrub trousers he was wearing and let them fall to the floor, then stood there, stark naked apart from some bandages and a knee brace.

Alex's mouth dropped open and his eyes widened.

173

"Oh my God, Conor! What are you trying to do to me? How am I supposed to control myself with you standing there looking like... Looking like... Fuck! Get dressed!" He pulled a set of police issue sweats from a bag. "I brought these because they're soft and stretchy. I wasn't sure how sore you would be." Underwear, socks and a pair of running shoes followed.

"If you could just hold the underwear, I can step into them. My knee doesn't bend much in this brace."

Now Alex was the one blushing. He got to his knees and held the stretchy shorts out with his eyes closed. Conor stepped into them trying not to laugh at Alex's screwed up face. "You can pull them up now, Alex."

"You're a fucking tease and I'd take you over my knee right here if I could." Alex maneuvered the underwear over Conor's knee brace then abandoned him. Conor tucked himself in, which was more difficult than usual because he was semi-hard. "I can manage the top but you're going to have to help with everything else, Alex."

Alex swore and started muttering. "So bloody unfair. Thrusting temptation in my face when I can't do anything about it. What have I done to deserve this? Fuck, fuck, fuck."

Conor enjoyed every minute. Quite apart from having Alex groveling at his feet, which would probably never happen again, he enjoyed tormenting his lover. It took his mind away from the dark memories that lurked too close to the surface for comfort.

"Wait here." Alex stalked out of the room, lips pressed tightly together, eyebrows creased into a frown. He returned, pushing a wheelchair and looking a lot more cheerful. Conor eyed the chair. "You don't expect me to get in that, do you?"

Alex patted the seat. "Revenge is sweet. Hospital policy says you have to ride out of here, so in you get. I'm driving."

"I can walk! I don't want to get in that thing, Alex." He felt like stamping his foot but didn't because he knew it would hurt.

"Well on this occasion, sweetheart, what you want doesn't matter. Now get in... Or I'll put you in."

Conor looked from Alex to the wheelchair and back again. It wouldn't be beyond Alex to handcuff him to the chair if he didn't do as he was told. Conor decided that it was a battle not worth fighting. He sat in the chair and tried not to pout as Alex wheeled him from the room.

Doctors and nurses kept stopping them to say goodbye. Even the cleaning lady came and patted Conor's hand and wished him well. She looked at Alex and nodded. "You look after him, he's such a sweetie."

Alex headed for the lift at speed.

"You can probably be arrested for dangerous driving with this thing, you know." Conor held on tightly.

"I just want you out of here. Two days and every female in the place wants to get in your pants! All you had to do was lie there and look pretty. You're mine."

Conor chuckled. "Could you be any more possessive? They were just being kind."

Alex did a wheelie with the chair as he turned it around inside the lift. "And you are such an innocent. Nobody needs as many bed baths as you were given in the last couple of days."

"Twice a day, Alex, that's hardly excessive, and I wasn't allowed to get up so it was necessary."

"Those nurses were drawing lots to see who got to apply that sponge, you know." Alex sounded so affronted that Conor burst out laughing. It was such a relief to be going home.

They reached the car park level and as the lift doors slid open Conor was greeted by a round of applause and a whole crowd of people from the station, complete with shiny foil balloons and enormous bunches of colorful flowers. Alex wheeled him into the center of the crowd of well-wishers and applied the brakes. Conor didn't know where to look. Sergeant Higgs crouched down next to him. "You're quite the hero, son. Everyone wanted to come by and say hello but the big bad boss here wouldn't let them visit while you were resting."

"I'm no hero. All I managed to do was crash my bike and fall into the hands of a psychopath. It was you guys who worked out where I was and came to the rescue."

Alex squeezed his shoulder gently. Higgs patted his knee. "You can play it down all you like, Detective, but a hero is what you are. Now get yourself well and come back to work because none of the others can make tea worth a damn."

Conor shrugged off the praise and answered a barrage of questions before he started to flag. He hadn't realized how quickly he would get tired. Recovery from his experience was going to take a bit longer than he'd hoped. He was actually starting to feel grateful that he was sitting down.

"That's enough, you lot!" Alex bellowed. "Conor needs to rest. Now get out of the way before I commit crime by wheelchair!"

The crowd gradually dispersed amid a hail of cheerful insults aimed at Alex, who manhandled misbehaving balloons and bouquets toward the car along with Conor's wheelchair. When they finally got to the vehicle, Conor heaved a sigh of relief. Alex gave him a strange look. He seemed nervous, vulnerable even. When he spoke, his voice was gruff. "The Rasputin operation is over, so you're under no obligation to stay with me anymore. However, I'm driving and I'm going back to my place where I intend to keep you until you are fully healed. Do you have a problem with that?"

"Kidnapped twice in one week—this is getting to be a habit. It doesn't sound like I have much choice?" Conor's lips twitched as he tried not to smile. He couldn't imagine being anywhere but with Alex.

"Very perceptive, you *don't* have a choice. Now get in the car and behave yourself." Conor caught the smile that Alex tried to hide. His man was just a big softy underneath all the alpha male posturing. "Yes, sir." Conor levered himself up and clambered awkwardly into the passenger seat. He pulled on the belt, trying not to wince as the strap pressed against his bandaged chest and shoulder. His pain medication must have been starting to wear off. He shut his eyes.

"I'm just going to return this contraption to the trolley park and then we can be off," Alex said cheerfully.

"This is a hospital, not a supermarket, Alex."

"Same difference. I hate both of them." He slammed the car door and wheeled the chair away. He was back in a couple of minutes cursing a sore ankle as he got behind the wheel. "Bloody chair fought back, just like those supermarket trolleys always do." He turned to Conor and concern flashed across his face, "Hey, are you okay?"

"I'm fine, just tired. It's ridiculous—all I've done is sleep for the last forty-eight hours and I'm still shattered."

"You've been through hell. You need to listen to your body and do as it tells you. We really have to work on your obedience, don't we?"

"I'm sure you'll enjoy that." Conor yawned.

The next thing he knew, Alex was gently shaking him awake. "Hey, we're home. Do you think you can walk to the house?"

"Sure, I'll be fine." Conor did wait for Alex to open the car door for him so that he didn't have to twist around too much. He swiveled on his arse and let Alex support him as he shuffled to the edge of the seat. He got his feet on the ground and unfolded his body carefully, finding his balance. His legs were really shaky but he was determined to get to the front door under his own steam. He took a couple of deep breaths and limped up the path.

Alex propped him up as he groped for his keys but the door opened before he could find them. Agnes hovered there with a welcoming smile. She hardly waited for Conor to get inside before she accosted him with a careful hug. "You are both such bad boys making me worry so much, and now look at you. Conor, you look like you've been trampled by a herd of cows." Between the hall and the kitchen, she fussed around, scolding Alex as if he was a rebellious teenager who'd been caught getting home after his curfew.

After a guided tour of the meals she had pre-prepared and left in the fridge and freezer for them, Agnes finally left. Alex breathed a sigh of relief. "She's worse than my mother!" But his voice betrayed the affection he felt for her. "I swear she makes me feel like a naughty ten-year-old most of the time."

Conor chuckled. "It's good for you. Someone needs to boss you around every now and then." He leaned against the kitchen counter. "Is it okay if I take a nap? I feel a bit woozy." Alex was immediately all over him, fussing just as much as Agnes. Fifteen minutes later Conor was propped up against a pile of pillows in bed and Alex was pressing pills and a glass of water into his hand.

"These are quite strong so they should help you sleep as well as deal with the pain I know you're in." Dutifully Conor swallowed the tablets and handed the glass back. Alex had helped him up the stairs, washed his face, helped him undress, then tucked him in.

He didn't want him to go. He felt stupidly vulnerable at the thought of being alone. He patted the bed. "Stay with me?" Alex didn't tease him at all. He just stripped off his clothes and climbed beneath the covers. Conor pressed against as much of Alex's hard body as he comfortably could and sighed happily. The painkillers were making him feel like he was floating and Alex was so warm... Conor drifted into sleep feeling safe and content.

He slept on and off for the next twenty-four hours. Alex was always around when he awoke, either in bed with him or hovering with comfort food and medication. Free from pain, Conor drifted peacefully in and out of vague, meaningless dreams. Eventually he woke feeling a lot more alert. He could hear Alex pottering in the kitchen so he drew in a deep breath and got out of bed. He hobbled to the bathroom and used the toilet with some relief that he could manage the simple task on his own. Turning on the shower, he wondered if he could manage to remove his knee brace without falling on his face. "Well, you're not going to find out until you try," he muttered and tackled the Velcro closures. The restrictive strapping fell away. "Oh! That's sooo good!" he exclaimed. Testing his knee gingerly he found he could put weight on it without too much pain. He wouldn't be running anywhere anytime soon but it didn't feel nearly as bad as he'd feared. Carefully he stepped beneath the shower and luxuriated in the feeling of hot water on his skin. Belatedly he realized that all his dressings were getting wet but then decided that they would have to be changed soon anyway. He did turn away from the spray so that his chest was protected a bit.

The water felt unbelievably good and Conor had no idea how long he stood there soaping and shampooing. He wanted to wash the scent of disinfectant from his skin. He didn't really want to get out of the shower at all but the water was starting to cool so he switched it off and went to squeeze the drips from his hair. His hands searched for length that wasn't there and suddenly everything came flooding back. Rasputin hacking at his hair, the insanity in the murderer's eyes as he sang and lifted his knife...

"What the fuck, Conor! I can't leave you alone for ten minutes, can I?" Alex threw open the shower door and helped him out, drawing him close in a soggy hug.

Conor took a couple of shuddering breaths and came back to reality. "Sorry, I felt so dirty and it doesn't hurt so much anymore."

"That's not what I mean and you know it." Alex wrapped him in a towel and began to pat gently. "Those flashbacks are going to be with you for a while. Little things will trigger them when you least expect it. It's normal. Post-traumatic stress. I just don't want you dealing with it alone." He finished drying and rubbed at Conor's hair a bit before kissing him lightly. "Come and lie on the bed so I

179

can change your bandages, they're all wet."

As Conor settled onto his back, Alex produced some underwear and helped him wriggle into them.

Alex sighed. "That's better. Jesus, Conor, it's more than a man should have to put up with, having you naked and not being able to touch."

Conor sniggered. "Did the doc say you had to keep your hands off me then?"

"No, but… You're hurt. Now keep still."

Conor lay quietly as Alex strapped the brace back around his knee. It didn't hurt when the dressings were peeled from his shoulder. Alex looked down at him. "I think that's healed well enough to leave exposed now. The grazes are pretty bad but it was surface damage. Same with the wound on your head. Like all scalp wounds, lots of dramatic bleeding but not as bad as it looked and the stitches will dissolve on their own."

Conor tensed as Alex started to remove the large square pads that were taped to the top of his chest. "How bad is it?" he whispered.

"You have seven cuts," Alex said bluntly. "They're not very deep. The doc thinks you'll have faint scars but nothing too scary. You have pale skin so they probably won't show unless you get a tan. At the moment, they are a bit gruesome — red, but knitted well. There's bruising too — quite the rainbow of colors." He ripped open some dressing packets. "Doc said these are special wound dressings — they'll allow the cuts to dry but prevent infection. Bates was proud of his equipment — all of the knives had been sterilized so you don't have to worry about that. I'll have to change the dressings every day for the next couple of weeks but the cuts are already looking much better."

"It aches a bit, across the top of my chest. I think the muscles were strained as well, from hanging there." Conor kept still as Alex taped the white squares in place. "Feels stiff."

"That makes two of us then," Alex muttered under his

breath, making Conor snort with laughter.

"Hey! No laughing at the medic! I can't help it if touching you turns me on." Conor sat up slowly. "How about you help me get dressed then and we go downstairs? I need to feel normal and I'm not going to do that hiding in the bedroom."

"Are you sure you're up to it?" Alex looked hopeful.

"Definitely. If you could find me some loose jeans so that they go over the brace." Conor looked ruefully at the bruising on his hip and thigh. "That bastard gave me quite a kicking."

"Here, you can wear a pair of mine, they're bigger." Alex threw him some worn jeans and a soft navy shirt then helped him dress. Conor managed most of it himself, insisting that he had to try. He didn't bother with socks — they weren't worth the struggle.

The two of them headed downstairs to the lounge and Conor settled onto the sofa while Alex went to get drinks and some sandwiches. They ate in front of the TV, catching up with the news. The Rasputin case was no longer the headline story but there was a piece about Bates undergoing some kind of psychological evaluation. Alex grunted. "Doesn't need a professional to work out that he's a psychopath." He got up and put their plates on the coffee table then switched off the set with an annoyed flourish of the remote.

Alex climbed into the armchair and sat with one knee pulled up, staring hard at Conor. "Are you in any pain? And please don't try to put on a brave face because I will know if you lie to me."

"My knee aches, but everything else is fine." Conor smiled and shifted his leg — the brace wasn't designed for comfort.

"Would you like some painkillers?" Alex asked.

He shook his head. "No. If I can't feel it how will I know when it's better? It's not that bad, really."

Alex fidgeted in his seat. He picked up a book and put it down again, got up and prodded at the fire with the poker, wandered over to the window and fiddled with the curtains. Conor watched him with calm amusement. Alex was always so self-assured — it was nice to know that there were some things that could upset his usual confident demeanor.

Conor took pity on him. "I won't break, Alex."

Alex had the grace to look sheepish. "Am I that transparent?"

Conor nodded. "I'm afraid so."

"I need to touch you so badly."

Conor smiled. "I'm fine, honestly. I'm more than happy for you to feel every inch if it will stop you bouncing off the walls like a toddler on a sugar high."

Alex put two more logs onto the fire then held out his hand. Conor took it and was pulled to his feet. Alex positioned him on the rug, "Stand here, in front of the fire. I don't want you to get cold."

"Why would I get cold?"

"Because I'm taking you at your word — I intend to check over every inch." Alex's smile was just a little bit wicked. Conor shivered as Alex stroked a few strands of hair away from his face to examine the cut that stretched along his hairline from his temple to the corner of his eyebrow. Alex let the hair fall back and circled behind him, brushing his fingers across the nape of Conor's neck. "I like your hair shorter, though I won't be recommending your barber to anyone else." He ran gentle fingers down the side of Conor's face then leaned in and kissed the point to the side of his eye on one side then the other. Before Conor could say anything Alex pressed a finger against his lips. "Don't speak. Don't move." It wasn't a request, it was a command. The real Alex had surfaced again and Conor trembled with desire.

The only ache Conor could feel was the pulsing throb of his cock, any other pain numbed by desire. He shivered as Alex kissed him with the merest brush of his lips then lapped at the soft part of one earlobe. Alex was apparently doing his best to hunt down every erogenous zone Conor possessed. Kisses traced the line of his neck until they met the barrier of his collar. Alex muttered his frustration and tugged Conor's shirt out of his waistband and began to undo buttons with remarkably steady fingers. Conor was impressed. Dexterity under pressure was not one of his talents.

Alex pushed the dark blue fabric of Conor's shirt back onto his shoulders and paused. The snowy white surgical dressings that Alex had applied were neatly taped in place along the top of Conor's chest. Alex's ice blue eyes seemed to chill even further until Conor touched his face reassuringly. Alex nodded and finished removing the shirt. Satisfied, Alex ran his hands down Conor's back, tracing the ridge of his spine, smoothing and stroking his skin. "Just like satin," he murmured.

Conor leaned into Alex's touch. If he were a cat he'd have been purring by now. His muscles twitched under Alex's caress, rippling beneath his skin as Conor shifted slightly.

Alex gripped Conor's waist and stroked the plains of his stomach with his thumbs. "Every bit of you is beautiful, Conor." Conor leaned in, begging for a kiss with his eyes. Alex obliged and this time wasn't so gentle. Conor responded fiercely, desperate to taste Alex while he could. When Alex pulled away Conor whimpered at the loss. He tried to steady his breathing but then Alex began to unbutton his fly and it was a lost cause. Because they were a size bigger than he would normally wear, Alex's jeans sat low on Conor's narrower hips. As Alex released the studs the jeans slipped downwards slightly. Alex ran his fingers beneath the denim, teasing and probing, gradually pushing downwards. He dropped to his knees and guided the fabric over Conor's brace until Conor was able to step out of the garment completely.

The fire crackled merrily but Conor didn't need its heat to stay warm. He felt like he was glowing from within, standing there, subjected to Alex's scrutiny. His rigid cock was uncomfortably restrained by his underwear and he couldn't wait for Alex to pull them down. Alex had other ideas. He ignored Conor's obvious discomfort and stroked the backs of his thighs instead.

Conor moaned pitifully. "Please, Alex, don't make me beg. I've been tortured once already this week."

Alex smirked. He maintained eye contact as he slid his hands into the back of Conor's trunks, grasped his arse and kneaded the cheeks firmly. When he brushed his fingertips across Conor's entrance it was all Conor could do not to scream his frustration. "Please, Alex! Touch me!"

Alex looked up from his position on the floor. "Who's in charge here, brat?"

Conor gulped. Words like that just made him harder. "You are, sir."

"That's right, so keep quiet or I'll gag you." He said it with a smile but Conor knew that he wasn't kidding. He clenched his jaw and scowled, which just made Alex grin even more. Conor debated playing the sympathy card and decided against it—there was no way he wanted Alex to stop and that would probably be the result of mentioning that he was still recovering. He watched the fire, attempting to focus on the flames rather than Alex's hands on his arse, but it was impossible. His underwear could have been on fire and still all he would feel were the light strokes across the curve of his backside and the feather-light grazing of his hole.

When Conor thought that he couldn't possibly take any more, Alex finally relented and pulled Conor's now damp underwear down allowing his straining cock to spring free. Conor's legs shook as he kicked the underwear away. He locked his knees, thankful for the support the brace gave him, and clasped his hands behind his back.

"Watch." Alex's command made Conor look down instantly. Alex circled the tip of Conor's aching cock with one finger, gathering the moisture that had collected there. Slowly Alex lifted it to his lips and lapped up the stickiness.

"Oh, that tastes good, but I think I need a bigger sample."
Then Conor did scream as Alex took him deep into his mouth.
At the same time he thrust his wet finger into Conor's arse.
He twisted in time with his sucking motion and Conor's
world disappeared. His eyes were open but he could only
see flashing swirls of light. Desperately, he grabbed some
of Alex's hair and held on. Pinned between Alex's questing
mouth and twisting finger Conor's unbraced knee buckled
as he came with force down Alex's throat.

Alex supported him and lowered him gently onto the
couch.

Gradually his vision cleared and he took a deep breath.
"Christ, Alex, are you trying to kill me? There's only so
much a man can take!"

Alex crouched in front of him and smiled wickedly. "Oh
believe me, I'm just getting started with you."

185

EVIL'S
EMBRACE

INVESTIGATING LOVE

Never underestimate the
power of obsession...

L M SOMERTON

Evil's Embrace

Excerpt

Chapter One

Detective Inspector Alex Courtney straightened his dark red spotted tie and smiled as he remembered the alternative use it had been put to just that morning. It certainly looked better wrapped around his boyfriend Conor's wrists than it did around Alex's neck. Neckties were an unfortunate necessity of his job and rank, though Alex had no clue how partial strangulation made him a better detective. Even the tie couldn't dampen his mood, however. His morning's adventures in the bedroom were not the only reason for the smile on his face. It had been four months to the day since his team had brought down the serial killer Rasputin, and he and Conor had finally found a space in their diaries to take some well-earned time off. Alex couldn't remember the last time he'd looked forward to a holiday so much. Just a few more hours and he would be heading for Cornwall and hopefully some late summer sun, with the most gorgeous man in the world.

Alex just had one more job to do. He closed and locked his office door then headed downstairs to the room his team occupied. He'd scheduled a meeting for the last half hour of the day so that he could escape immediately afterwards. When he got there, they were all waiting expectantly. Alex was on the verge of making up some excuse and just leaving, but he met Sergeant Higgs' kindly gaze and steeled his resolve.

"Make yourselves comfortable, lads, I've got a few things I need to say." Alex perched on the edge of a table and waited while the four men in front of him settled into their seats. "First of all, I want to thank you all. The last four months have been challenging to say the least. I'm happy to say that the Rasputin case has now been handed over to the legal team and we can forget about it until they need us in court. Several small forests have been sacrificed to the paperwork that went with this case and I really appreciate your dedication to making sure we got it right."

There were a few low grunts and a smattering of applause. "Now, I've got used to the constant complaints from you all about Conor's absence. Apparently the quality of the tea has reached rock bottom and rebellion is brewing along with the over-stewed tea bags. Anyone would think I'm keeping Conor away from work deliberately."

"We know you want to wrap him up in cotton wool, boss, but he'd be much better off here with us. You know — straight back in the saddle and all that," Sergeant Higgs said in a gruff voice.

"I'm really touched by how much support Conor is getting from you all. He's obviously made quite an impression."

"And not just on us, boss!" That comment brought a chorus of chuckles.

Alex held back a grin. "I don't need to remind you that Conor hasn't just fallen off a horse and the psychological damage of being held and tortured by a serial killer is not something to be underestimated. However, I am pleased to tell you that Conor will be rejoining you when we return from leave."

"Well, it's about fucking time."

Alex fought down some persistently flapping butterflies in his stomach before saying, "You all know that Conor and I are together. Neither of us wants that to interfere with the way this team works. If any of you think that our relationship will cause problems, Conor will request an immediate transfer to another team with no hard feelings. We've talked about it a lot and neither of us will be happy unless you are all comfortable. I know none of you are homophobic, that's not where I'm coming from. I'd be saying the same if one of you was a woman that I was involved with."

That got some low chuckles.

"Okay, that didn't come out quite right, but you know what I mean!"

Higgs coughed and looked at his team mates for their approval to speak up on their behalf.

Alex clenched his fist tightly as Higgs began, "Boss, you can stop worrying. We all want the lad to stay. He's a bloody good detective and he fits in well. None of us gives a shit what you do on your own time, and to be frank, you've been slightly less of a bastard since you've been with him. You work him harder than the rest of us put together, so I suppose the question is more whether he'll put up with you?" Higgs' face cracked into a grin.

Alex remembered how to breathe and sucked some oxygen into his lungs. "Well, that remains to be seen. They reckon a holiday is a test of any relationship, don't they? After two weeks in each other's company Conor may well be ready to kill me."

"Just don't expect us to pick up the investigation, boss!"

"They're going to the arse end of Cornwall — don't think they even have a police force down there, do they?"

"Course they do, there's loads of crime. Seagulls pinching

your sandwiches on the beach, aggravated assault by crabs when you dip a toe in the wrong rock pool—it's all going on down there. Highly dangerous."

Alex groaned. "I've already spoken to the boss. The Chief Inspector, and I quote, said she 'couldn't give a rat's arse about who is doing what unless it's against the law'. All she's interested in is our case closure rate."

"Stop worrying about us and get off home. We'll look forward to seeing both of you back at the coal face in two weeks." Higgs walked Alex out to the front desk and shook his hand at the door. "I'm proud of you, lad. You and Conor both. Now go and have the break you deserve."

Alex drove home feeling almost euphoric. All his worries about the case, Conor's recovery and the possibility that Conor might have to transfer divisions were gone. At least temporarily. Less than an hour later he had showered, changed into comfy jeans and a pale blue T-shirt and was sitting at the counter in his kitchen as Conor served up their dinner. Detective Conor Trethuan was, in Alex's humble and totally biased opinion, the most beautiful man he'd ever set eyes on. Sipping a glass of nicely chilled orange juice he examined Conor from head to toe. Dark, almost black hair, nicely tousled—check. Gorgeous green eyes shaded by long dark lashes—check. The hottest body he'd ever had the luck to get his hands on—check. Conor put a plate of sea bass and vegetable rice in front of him—it could have been a fish paste sandwich for all Alex cared—and gave him a pained look.

"I wish you wouldn't look at me like that." There was a slight tinge of pink on Conor's defined cheekbones.

"Like what?" Alex acted the innocent.

"As if you want to rip my clothes off and toss me over your shoulder like some marauding Viking invader." Conor clambered onto his stool and began to eat.

"Oh, like that. Well it would be difficult not to look at you that way, because that's exactly what I *would* like to do to you. A bit of marauding in the evening is always a good thing." Alex mulled over that idea as he ate. "Mmm. This is delicious. Of course I wouldn't be able to stop there. Ravishing would have to follow."

Conor nibbled at his bottom lip. "And what exactly would that entail?"

"Well... A gag, of course, and some nice thick rope to tie you down with."

Conor rolled his eyes. "Of course."

"You'd fight me all the way, obviously, so I'd have to subdue you with a good paddling. Show you who's boss."

Conor shifted on his stool and Alex gave him an evil grin. "I do love it when a captive struggles."

"Eat your dinner, Alex."

"Yes, love." Alex could clearly see the hard edge of Conor's cock through the fabric of his jeans. He decided that they would continue this theme later, in the bedroom.

Alex concentrated on the meal, which was really tasty. He decided to change the subject and let Conor stew for a while. Something Higgs had said back at the station was playing on his mind. He stabbed at his food and asked, "Do you think I'm too hard on you, at work?"

Conor raised one dark eyebrow slightly. "I'd rather you were hard in me."

Alex choked on his mouthful of rice and grinned. "Later. That's a promise. Seriously, though, Higgs reckons I treat you far worse than the rest of them." He twirled his fork through his fingers. "Is he talking out of his arse or am I really that much of a bastard?"

Conor gazed at him. "He's right, you do have a tendency to treat me like the team skivvy. But be honest, if someone else was the youngest, least experienced member of the team would you be any different?"

Alex shook his head, feeling a bit sheepish.

"Well then. That's good—you should be your own grouchy self. At work you're the boss, not my boyfriend, and I don't expect anything else."

"Grouchy?" Alex pretended to be hurt. Conor ignored

him. "Definitely. Did you ever watch *Sesame Street* as a kid?"

"Where the hell are you going with this? Of course I did — that's the one with the weird yellow bird thing, isn't it?"

"That's the one. Remember the grumpy green monster that lived in a dustbin?"

Alex growled.

"Oscar the Grouch. That's you at work."

Alex could see that Conor was desperately trying not to laugh and it was infectious. He wanted to laugh too. He tried hard to stop himself but he couldn't. He was happy, he was on holiday — he laughed until tears sprang from the corners of his eyes, and Conor looked at him as if he was totally crazy.

Conor cleared their plates away and made coffee.

"Since you've been off work, you've become quite the domestic goddess, haven't you?" Alex teased.

"It's kept me from going insane with boredom. Are you complaining?"

"Not at all. Your cooking's getting pretty accomplished."

"And you're the beneficiary! I actually quite like trying out new recipes on you and Agnes loves teaching me."

"She loves having you around. You could probably slouch on the sofa watching TV all day and she'd still fawn over you like a new puppy."

Alex hopped off his stool and went to rummage in the kitchen drawer that contained an assortment of odds and ends that didn't have a home anywhere else.

"What are you looking for?" Conor asked.

"I'm sure they're in here somewhere," Alex muttered to himself, pushing aside batteries, elastic bands and a pot of odd nails and screws. "Yes! Success. Come over here, sweetheart." He steered Conor around the counter, took hold of his arm and pushed his left sleeve up, revealing the smooth band of dark grey metal that sat snugly around Conor's narrow wrist. Alex brandished the small pair of pliers that he'd dug out of the drawer.

191

"The tracker in this bracelet may not have saved your life in quite the way I intended, but it certainly helped. It gave us a clue as to where you might be. The chip had a limited lifespan, though, so it won't be transmitting anymore — would you like me to cut the band off?"

Alex played with Conor's hand and looked at him steadily. As much as Alex wanted to keep the bracelet in place, the choice had to be Conor's. "You want me to keep it on, don't you? Why? It doesn't work and you don't need to keep track of me anymore anyway." Conor demonstrated the intuition that made him such a good detective.

"That's a matter of opinion," Alex said under his breath as he met Conor's curious gaze.

"I know it makes me sound like a possessive freak, but I like that you can't take it off. It ties you to me... Does that sound weird?"

Conor nibbled at his lower lip. "You're doing that Dom thing again, aren't you? One of these days I just know I'm going to come home and find you waiting for me in a black leather harness, brandishing a whip."

Alex snorted, "You wish."

Conor blinked and cast his eyes down. Just that simple action had Alex's cock misbehaving in a very distracting way.

"Maybe," Conor whispered as he picked up the pliers from the counter and slipped them back into the drawer. "I think I'm getting off lightly by keeping this on — I'm surprised you don't want to weld a collar around my neck."

"If it wasn't for the job I'd certainly have a nice wide strip of leather padlocked here by now." Alex demonstrated by stroking Conor's throat with the back of his fingers.

Conor swallowed, and Alex followed his Adam's apple as it moved.

"I think you like that idea, don't you?"

Conor ducked his head and rested it on Alex's shoulder. "Even if I did, I definitely wouldn't tell you."

"You don't need to say it, love, I can see it in your face."

He smiled even though Conor couldn't see his expression. "A collar is a symbol of ownership. Maybe I can't have my mark permanently around your neck, but this wristband does the job almost as well. I put it there and you can't take it off. The principle is the same."

The slight tremor that shook Conor's frame told Alex that the idea had been well received and that made his world an even more perfect place to be.

It was cool enough in the evenings for a fire to feel pleasant, so Alex and Conor took their coffee into the lounge. Conor had already laid the fire and it didn't take much coaxing to bring it to life. Soon they had a nice blaze going and the room warmed quickly. Alex took a seat at one end of the sofa and Conor curled up against him, giving Alex a nice contented feeling.

"You know, I'm going to have to go home at some point. I've been here for months and I do have my own place."

Alex scowled as Conor broached a subject that they had both been avoiding since Alex had brought Conor back from the hospital.

"Is that what you want?" Alex asked, sounding grumpy even to his own ears. He felt hurt and disappointed.

Conor leaned into him and the affection was reassuring. "I just assumed..."

"What?"

"That you would want your own space back eventually. It was good of you to let me stay here while I was mending, but I'm all better now."

Alex pulled Conor closer. "What I want is you here with me. This is your home now. No arguments – you can pack up the other place and move in here permanently." Alex knew he sounded dictatorial but he didn't care. The idea of Conor living anywhere else was intolerable.

"You can't just order me around, Alex." Conor sounded indignant, but he wasn't very convincing and he didn't make any attempt to pull away.

Alex narrowed his eyes. "Disobedience has consequences.

You really are a slow learner, aren't you?"

Alex enjoyed the little tremble that reverberated through Conor's body and couldn't fail to notice that his lover's cock was making an interesting ridge in his trousers.

"Perhaps I'm just not getting enough positive reinforcement?"

"Well that's something I can help you with." Alex looked pointedly towards the stairs and Conor got up meekly. "Lessons can best be delivered in the bedroom." Alex stood and crowded Conor towards the stairs. "Move quicker."

Conor's head was spinning. Alex had just asked him to move in with him permanently and now he was giving a damn convincing demonstration of just how dominant he could be. Conor was in no doubt that there would be a lot more of this to come if they shared a home on a more permanent basis. That thought had him hard and aching as he backed towards the bed, trembling with anticipation.

Alex advanced towards him, taking his shirt off and throwing it aside. His bare skin gleamed golden and his muscles rippled. There was so much strength contained within that gorgeous body, Conor felt totally safe when they were together, even when Alex was looking as intimidating as he did at that moment. Alex grasped Conor's collar and ripped his shirt open—his buttons flew in all directions, scattering like hail against the furniture. The torn fabric slid from his shoulders but he didn't have time to mourn the destruction of his clothing because Alex was already working on his lower half, yanking down his trousers and underwear leaving him naked and breathless.

"On your knees."

Conor only resisted for a second as Alex pushed him down and spread his knees apart with a foot until he was satisfied.

"Hands behind your back."

The position was utterly submissive but Conor refused to bow his head. He met Alex's gaze defiantly. His cock

194

betrayed how much he enjoyed Alex's dominant behaviour, rock hard and gleaming with pre-cum. Alex took a black silk scarf off the peg on the back of the bedroom door and smiled with evil intent. Conor's eyes widened but he didn't fight it as Alex tied the scarf tightly around them and his world went dark. He heard the metallic slide of a zipper and the soft rustle of fabric. A floorboard creaked slightly. He pictured Alex removing the rest of his clothing and wished he could see. It wasn't fair that Alex could watch him, naked and kneeling, while he was deprived of the pleasure of admiring Alex's body.

"Fuck, you are breathtaking! I could come just looking at you." Alex's voice was as rough as gravel.

"That would be a disgraceful waste." Conor shifted on his knees. He wanted desperately to touch himself but he resisted and kept his hands together behind his back. If he broke the unstated rules, Alex would only extend his torment further, and when they played, his body belonged to Alex. Touching was out of the question. He locked his fingers together as a preventative measure, just in case they strayed without his knowledge.

"On your feet." That sounded like a nice, simple order, but getting up with his hands behind his back wasn't easy.

Conor rose awkwardly, and Alex guided him to the bed where he positioned him on his back, legs spread wide, knees bent. "Put your hands above your head and keep them there."

Conor complied and wondered if his entire body was as pink as his face must be. He felt so exposed. The mattress dipped a little and he knew that Alex was kneeling in the space that remained between his legs. Alex's cock brushed against him and it became apparent that Conor wasn't the only one craving skin on skin contact.

"I've got a little present for you."

Conor drew in his breath sharply as something cold and metallic was draped across his chest. He wondered what kind of clamps Alex had selected from his collection. Alex's warm breath caressed his torso then Alex licked one nipple before sucking and biting until it ached. Conor arched his back, thrusting his cock into Alex's abdomen, desperate for some friction. Alex edged back, denying him. Conor bit back a curse of frustration then tensed as Alex began screwing a chilly clamp to his hardened nipple. *Not the ones with biting little teeth then.* These were smooth and unyielding. Not sprung, Alex could tighten them as much as he wanted and they would not give. As the clamp compressed his nipple, the initial pain intensified before fading to a tingling throb of pleasure that radiated downwards towards his groin. Conor still couldn't help swearing as Alex repeated the process on the other bud.

"Bloody hell! That hurts."

"I'm sure it does, but it looks perfect. There's a pretty chain linking the two clamps."

The chain was immediately tugged in demonstration, and Conor writhed beneath Alex's touch, his fingers clenching and unclenching as pulses of pain shot through his body.

"Bastard! Stop! It's too much, Alex."

"It's too much, Sir. Please address me properly." The chain was tweaked again. "We talked about safe words just last week. Remind me of yours."

Conor panted. It was hard to focus. "Rose to slow down, thorn to stop, Sir."

"Good. Until you use those words, I get to decide what's too much for you. I think we have a way to go yet."

"Sir! Please!" Conor didn't really know what he was asking for. The pain felt so good. He was desperate for Alex to fill him. He needed to come so much it was all-consuming. His cock throbbed just as much as his nipples and he didn't want it to stop.

Alex's hands on his hips gave Conor hope that relief would come soon. His body lifted a little and the cool blunt head of Alex's cock pressed against him. Conor abruptly remembered that Alex hadn't used any lube—penetration was going to hurt. He gasped as Alex pushed until just the head of his cock breached Conor's resistant opening. There was just a slight burn with the stretch, but Conor trusted Alex, and he didn't fight him. He was rewarded when Alex began to stroke him. His cock, already hard and heavy, jerked in agitation. He was so close to the edge and yet Alex knew exactly when to stop. The touch disappeared and Alex's cock retreated, to be replaced by two fingers coated with lube. Conor whimpered as Alex thrust his fingers forwards and scissored them. A third was soon added and Conor pleaded shamelessly, repeating the word "please" over and over. But Alex was merciless. He didn't speed up. He controlled Conor's body with his touch, holding him over the abyss until Conor's head swam with sensation, with pleasure, with raw need.

Conor was left empty as Alex removed his fingers and pulled him up farther against his thighs. Conor had no time to scream as Alex thrust forward in one smooth motion until he was buried deep. He just had enough coordination left to pull his knees back, allowing Alex to drive deeper. The blindfold seemed to magnify the sensations that Conor was experiencing—the pleasure was almost unbearable. Alex plunged into him harder, grazing his prostate with every stroke. Conor gripped the sides of the bed and forgot how to breathe. Time stood still. There was nothing but Alex, in him, over him, possessing him. The second Alex relented and took a firm hold of his cock, Conor succumbed and covered Alex's hand with the results of the most intense orgasm he'd ever felt. Alex continued to pound into him until his own explosive release followed, filling Conor's passage with liquid heat.

For a few seconds the only sound was of heavy breathing. Then Alex rolled to one side of the bed and grunted, "Holy fuck, that was incredible!"

He turned Conor gently and kissed him passionately, using the distraction to remove the nipple clamps. Conor yelped—having the clamps removed was always more painful than when they were put on and it felt as if his nipples were on fire. The kisses helped, but not quite enough. Alex chuckled and pulled the blindfold away from Conor's eyes.

"I hope you've learnt your lesson?" Alex was smirking. "I certainly enjoyed delivering it."

Conor pouted. "I'm afraid I'm incorrigible, you'll no doubt have to remind me again very soon."

"I don't doubt it." Alex rolled away, flicking a tender nipple. "Those screw clamps looked good on you."

Conor winced. "I'm sure they'd look good on you too!"

"Not something you're ever likely to see, though."

"I can dream." The visual alone would be enough to give Conor some very enjoyable dreams.

"You didn't mind, though? I didn't check with you first…"

Conor leaned over his anxious lover and stroked sweat-dampened blond hair away from his eyes. "Of course not. I'm yours and whatever you want to try is fine with me." He kissed him tenderly. "And I certainly don't expect you to ask first — where's the fun in that?"

"I just…"

"Hey, I have a safe word and I know how to use it. I'm not an idiot, Alex. I don't believe you'd ever take me further than I want to go, but this is all new to me. I think finding my limits is going to be a lot of fun, so stop worrying."

After a few minutes of companionable silence he said, "I'm really looking forward to our holiday, to spending some time with you."

Alex hugged him close. "Mm. I've not taken any time off since the start of the Rasputin investigation, I can't wait. Two whole weeks of just you and me. My idea of heaven. I like having a boyfriend with a holiday home!"

Conor snuggled against Alex's shoulder. "When my grandparents died I sold their house but they also had this small cottage in Cornwall that I kept on. I usually go down there at this time of year, do a bit of maintenance before the holiday season, surf a bit. I've never taken anyone else there before."

"I'm honoured. It's in quite an isolated spot, isn't it?"

"It's not that far from the nearest village, but it's well hidden. It's pretty basic—and a good ten minutes' walk from the track that leads to the road. It dates back to the eighteenth century and it still has no central heating or mains electricity. It belonged to the local riding officer and has private access to a small cove that was the haunt of smugglers at the time. I spent all my summers there as a child and it was a great adventure."

"Well, it's important to you and that makes it important to me. I want you to show me everything. All the places you went when you were younger."

Conor breathed in Alex's familiar scent. He felt warm, happy and relaxed. Being with Alex made him feel cherished, something he'd missed since his grandparents had passed away. Two weeks together, away from the places that came with memories of Rasputin, was just what they both needed.

"I really need to take a shower. You've made me all sticky." Conor reluctantly rolled away from Alex.

"I'll give you a choice..." Alex sounded very serious.

"A choice about what?"

"Where I fuck you next. You can let me add to the stickiness right here, or you can bend over for me in the shower. What's it to be?"

Conor gave Alex's arm a gentle slap. "You really know how to romance a man, don't you?"

"Are you saying you don't want me without hearts and flowers?" Alex pouted like a three-year-old.

Conor stroked his chest. "I want you however you come, Alex Courtney, but you know that being a Dom means you get to make all the difficult decisions, don't you?"

"Where did you get that idea from?" Alex chuckled.

"Research. Detective, remember?"

"Ah. I see. Well in that case, get on your hands and knees. Your arse is mine. How about that for decisive?"

More books from
L.M. Somerton

Book one in the Tales from the Edge series

When you reach the edge, you can't avoid taking a leap of faith.

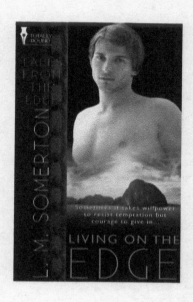

Book two in the Tales from the Edge series

Sometimes it takes willpower to resist temptation but courage to give in.

Book one in the Wyverns series

Not all cages have bars.

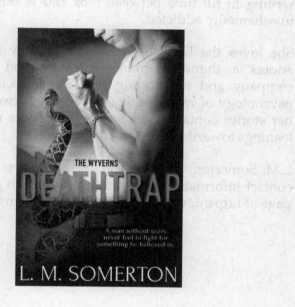

THE WYVERNS

DEATHTRAP

A man without scars
never had to fight for
something he believed in.

L. M. SOMERTON

Book two in the Wyverns series

*A man without scars never had to fight for something he
believed in.*

About the Author

L.M. Somerton

Lucinda lives in a small village in the English countryside, surrounded by rolling hills, cows and sheep. She started writing to fill time between jobs and is now firmly and unashamedly addicted.

She loves the English weather, especially the rain, and adores a thunderstorm. She loves good food, warm company and a crackling fire. She's fascinated by the psychology of relationships, especially between men, and her stories contain some subtle (and some not so subtle) leanings towards BDSM.

L.M. Somerton loves to hear from readers. You can find contact information, website details and an author profile page at https://www.pride-publishing.com/